MURDER AT HALE ALOHA

I jerked the poker from her lax fingers and stepped back, moving my own hand up to the handle where I now had a weapon between us.

"Why, Ingrid?" I cried. "Why?"

She stared at me. "Why what?"

"You know what!" I yelled, brandishing the poker as menacingly as I could. "Why did you kill my Aunt Tess?"

THE MYSTERY OF ALOHA HOUSE

by Lee Roddy

A Chime Suspense

David C. Cook Publishing Co.

ELGIN, ILLINOIS—WESTON, ONTARIO

FIRST EDITION
February, 1981

Cover design and illustration by Graphic Communications, Inc.
ISBN 0-89191-293-2
LC 80-66587

To my sisters-in-law:

Jane Roddy

Vivian Roddy

Sue Roddy

Chapter One

Every time I hear thunder drum across a blackened sky and see sheet lightning suddenly illuminate the night, I remember Aloha House.

It seems to me, looking back after more than ten years, that even the weather fought against my entering Aloha House that first time. The memories of the strange old mansion in Hawaii's rain forests surged through me tonight in the midst of a rare California thunder and lightning storm. The intense lightning and the drumming sounds that followed took me back, very unwillingly, to the day when I first saw the gloomy Victorian monstrosity that was to plunge me into such fearful danger. I was barely nineteen and all alone in the world. Well, almost. . . .

"Hale Aloha is just around the next bend," my Great-Aunt Tess said as the ancient family car wound its way deeper into the lush, yet almost overbearing, rain forest. The narrow black strip of asphalt we were traveling seemed lost in the surprising jungle that lurked just outside Honolulu's colorful and romantic lights.

Great-Aunt Tess squeezed my hand reassuringly, but I could see that her eyes were clouded with concern. The sense of foreboding, which had oozed around my heart at the airport, squeezed me tighter.

The tall Hawaiian driver in the front seat shifted the gears down again as the car approached yet another steep incline. His name was Kekeochi, he had told me, but everyone called him K. He had met me in the airport with a muscular hug—the typical Hawaiian welcome—and placed a lei of tiny vanda orchids around my neck.

The jungle seemed to close around us as the sky became darker and darker.

"The weather! Aunt Tess, what's happening to the beautiful ice-cream clouds?"

Tess's intensely blue eyes probed the lowering darkness, which seemed to settle over us like a canopy.

"It's the trees, Meganne, dear," she assured me. "We've climbed up behind Tantalus and Roundtop, far above Honolulu, into the forests of the Koolau Range. You know this is semitropical climate, so these jungle-like trees and vines are natural."

Her words were logical, yet somehow they didn't reassure me. I glanced out the open windows at the immense trees closing over us. The heavy trailing vines seemed to form a thickening net—and yet it wasn't the creeping jungle about us that concerned me.

"No, Aunt Tess," I said emphatically, "It's the weather! When I landed at Honolulu, the sky was perfectly clear and the most magnificent blue! Diamond Head was green, and beautiful white clouds like homemade vanilla ice cream floated above the ocean. But now look at it!"

We came to a momentary break in the canopy of rain forest. Far below, to our right, there was a flash of the city. It nestled between the collapsed volcanic landmark of Diamond Head and the splash of water that marked Pearl Harbor. I'd studied everything I could find on Hawaii after making an impulsive decision to visit my only living relatives, so I knew approximately where we were. But it was the sea that registered on my mind in the second before the old vehicle crawled back into the forest and shadows leaped to join us in the rusty car.

The ocean had been a beautiful blue green fading to a deep purple beyond the shoreline to the horizon. Immense black clouds were rising far to the south, beyond Diamond Head. They rose from the sea like some monstrous black beast creeping upon the fluorescent white clouds high overhead.

"*Kona* coming," the driver said. My blue eyes met his dark brown ones in the rearview mirror. "Ho! Big storm come soon, sistah!"

Tess explained, "K means that the south wind called a *kona* is bringing a threat of heavy rain. But it's nothing to be alarmed about, my dear! Usually, of course, we have what my sister calls 'champagne showers' with rainbows where you can see both ends at once, but those come with the trade winds."

"*Kona* bring planty big storm, sistah!" K repeated emphatically, steering through the darkened rain forest where the dense green undergrowth was now brushing the car.

"K, please don't lapse into that dreadful pidgin English! You don't need to impress my great-niece with your native background. I'm sure she's already noticed that you can speak perfectly good English when you wish."

Tess's words sounded like a rebuke, but her bright blue eyes sparkled above the wrinkled parchment covering her bony cheeks. I suspected there was a deep respect and understanding between the tall driver and the frail woman. Aunt Tess was seventy-five, I knew, and K wasn't more than twenty-five, but I felt a bond between the employer and employee.

"Aloha House," K said, nodding his head toward the end of the twisting blacktop road that unwound through the rain forest.

"Where?" I cried, leaning forward across the top of the backseat. "I don't see anything."

"There!" K said.

The great tent of trees and vines suddenly stopped. The car made the final turn. Beyond the immense iron gate that barred our way I glimpsed a huge Victorian house of somber battleship gray. A complex exterior arrangement of roofs melded into a series of gables, towers, and balconies. I'd seen something like it in San Francisco, and recognized the house as a combination of architecture. The roof line, with a "witch's cap" tower, and the general detailing were Queen Anne; the fretwork on the roof was Second Empire, as was the front tower with balcony.

I'd fallen in love with San Francisco's quaint Victorian homes, which someone had romantically christened, "painted ladies." But this monstrosity was gloomy and foreboding—a gray blob of homely wood intruding into the loveliness of Hawaii's natural beauty.

K slid out of the driver's side to unlock the iron gate.

Once he was beyond hearing, Aunt Tess's tight grip on my arm jerked my eyes from the mansion. "Meganne, dear," the old woman whispered with intensity, "something's happened since you called. You must get away from here as quickly as possible!"

I looked into the lined gentle face. The light in Tess's eyes had gone out, and I saw a bright point of fear in them.

"Why?" I managed to murmur.

"Please, Meganne! Don't ask questions! Not of me. Not of anyone. Especially my sister. And whatever you do, make some excuse and return to the Mainland as quickly as you possibly can!"

I blinked, trying to understand the sudden change in the dear old woman. "When I called you ten days ago and asked if I could come visit for a while, you said—."

"I know! I know! But that was before—."

"Before what?"

"Shh! K's coming back!"

The tall, slender driver slid under the wheel and eased the car through the gate. It had been made a long time ago, I guessed, when horse-drawn vehicles and even automobiles had been narrower. The rusted sides of the sedan barely cleared the black volcanic stones that had been shaped and fitted into the solid wooden gateposts.

"Ho!" K cried as he set the hand brake again. "All wind stop. Still as the dead now. *Kona* come sure!"

He walked past our open windows and started pulling the iron gates toward each other, one from either side, so they met in the middle. I twisted in my seat to watch him, but my whisper was to Tess.

"What in the world—?"

"Please, Meganne! I'll tell you more when we're alone. But promise me you'll not stay any longer than a few days!"

"Aunt Tess, I came here for some specific answers to some important questions that have nearly ruined my life a couple of times! I've got to know some things before I can even think of returning!"

The old woman squeezed my hand hard. "Trust me, Meganne!"

K returned after locking the gate. He got into the car and eased it forward along a badly pitted and unrepaired strip of blacktop. Giant trees lined the road on either side, with bougainvillaea in bright reds, purples, and pinks, relieving the somber gloom of the shadowed driveway.

"Ho! You like Hale Aloha, Miss Fields?"

"It's . . . different from what I expected," I replied

cautiously as the car moved closer to the mansion.

"You understand the words, *Hale Aloha*, Miss Fields?"

"Holly? Does it mean hollyhock?"

"No flower! *Hale* is Hawaiian for 'house.' Said same way as flower. Aloha means hello, good-bye, and love, you know. But this Hale Aloha means 'house of love.' "

"How . . . unusual."

"You stay a long time?" K's eyes again searched mine in the mirror.

It was an opportunity to tell Tess something she needed to know. "I don't know, K. Perhaps. You see, I spent every dime I had to get here."

I felt Tess make a slight movement against my shoulder, but she said nothing. Neither did K. He eased the car forward, past a high natural fence of flowering red and white oleanders.

My eyes took in as much of the old mansion as possible, but my mind was tumbling with sudden unanswered questions. I barely saw the tall, native stone chimneys soaring above the steep gabled roofs. Below were complicated exteriors with strange protrusions.

The car stopped. I was immediately aware of the total silence. The sweet, warm trade winds that had rattled palm fronds, ferns, hedges, and vines were gone. The air was heavy, oppressive. Once, when I was a little girl, I'd visited the Midwest with my parents and experienced a great quiet just before a terrible storm. The memory flickered into my mind as I stepped out of the car door.

I was surprised that no one came out of the house to meet us. I stepped onto the lush green lawn and turned uncertainly toward the steep marble stairs that led up to a small porch surrounded by fluted Corinthian columns.

"Meganne, my dear," Tess said as K lifted her wheelchair from the trunk, "remember your Aunt Marian is older than I, and she doesn't hear as well as she might. She hasn't heard us drive up, I suspect."

I looked at Tess with curiosity. Was she trying to reassure me about the lack of hospitality, or was she trying to tell me something? I'd never liked Aunt Marian. On the occasions when she had visited my mother, who was her niece, and my father, I'd been unbending to her blunt-spoken will. She had spoken sharply to me, which had only made me more stubborn. I still hadn't gotten over that "cussed streak," as my father had called it.

K had lifted Tess from the car and helped her into the wheelchair before I heard the mansion's front door squeak open. I glanced up the worn marble stairs, past the chipped, peeling gray paint on newel posts, balusters, and handrails. The decaying elegance of the home was echoed in the appearance of the woman at the top of the short flight of steps.

The daylight was fading, and deep shadows had squeezed into the porch. But in the dimness I could see a thin, prim woman nearing eighty.

I hesitated, then started up the steps toward the undisputed matriarch of a family that had all predeceased her except for Tess and me.

Marian's cool voice stopped me. "So," she said, "you've come, Meganne Fields!"

I was uncertain of what to do or say. Great-Aunt Marian did not smile, did not reach out her arms to embrace me, or even extend her hand.

"Yes," I said firmly, "I've come."

Chapter Two

Aunt Marian's body seemed to be so fragile it was almost lost under the out-of-style, frayed, and faded muumuu she wore. Her garment was nothing like the colorful, brightly patterned Mother Hubbard that had become popular with jetting tourists. It wasn't that she couldn't afford clothes, I knew. She looked like she was wearing something that had come from the bottom of a missionary barrel.

"You're looking well," I said uncertainly, standing on the top step and waiting for some sign of welcome.

"Yes, thank you. I am well. Sorry about your mother."

That was a hopeful sign. "Thanks," I murmured.

Aunt Marian continued to look at me. I was just stubborn enough to meet her hard blue eyes full on. She studied me through black-rimmed bifocals, which didn't lessen her severe look. She reminded me of a stern, old-fashioned schoolteacher. Her hair was graying but apparently touched up with brown. The result was a grizzled, mousy color with dozens of loose strands straying untidily in all directions.

Her eyes slid down the marbled steps. "K, get my sister

up the side ramp as quickly as possible. It's going to storm, I'm afraid. Quickly, now!"

Tess gave me a warning look as she was wheeled rapidly around the side of the house.

"K will also bring in your bags, Meganne," Marian said. "We're looking for a practical nurse to take care of my sister. But for now, K does very nicely."

"You must meet the others," she continued, opening the rusted screen door and motioning me through. The dimly lit hallway smelled of age, mildew, and mold.

"Tutu," Marian said as a heavy door opened and an enormous brown skinned woman stuck her head into the gloomy hallway, "this is my grandniece, Meganne Fields. Meganne, this is Tutu Kahama, our housekeeper."

The Hawaiian woman was at least six feet tall and weighed over three hundred pounds. She wore a tent-sized muumuu of brilliant red flowers on a colorful yellow and white background. She jiggled as she lumbered ponderously toward me. I was surprised to be engulfed in immense brown arms and crushed into a great swelling bosom.

"Welcome, Meganne! Welcome and aloha!"

Tutu released me and smiled warmly. That was my idea of a Hawaiian greeting, but it had come from a stranger.

"I'm glad to meet you, Tutu," I said.

"*Tutu* means 'grandmother' in Hawaiian," Aunt Marian said brusquely, "Tutu's been with us many years. You'll meet her husband later. And their adopted daughter, Malia, among others."

"Others?" I asked.

"Employees, friends, and neighbors, of course, Meganne. We had another servant, a practical nurse who took care of my sister the last year or so. But she is gone now . . ."

There was something about the way Aunt Marian mentioned the practical nurse that prompted me to ask what had happened.

She explained briefly. "Alice—that was her American name—died last week in an unfortunate accident."

I remembered Tess's recent warning. "How did it happen?"

Aunt Marian shrugged. "She knew enough about termites to never trust an old wooden railing. She leaned on it too hard."

Tutu's smile vanished. "Alema tripped; your sister herself—."

"My sister doesn't see well, Tutu!" Aunt Marian met my eyes and answered the question there. "She fell to her death on the rocks below. Be careful when you walk along the seaward side of the yard, Meganne. We're perched right on top of a precipice."

I looked at Aunt Marian and concluded there was something she wasn't telling me. And she wasn't going to let Tutu say anything, either.

Tutu turned away and vanished through a door at the far end of the corridor. I heard cups and saucers as Aunt Marian opened the nearest door. She stepped through and I followed like a schoolgirl.

The parlor, as Aunt Marian explained, rarely got much use. We walked on through, passing a stone fireplace so large I could have walked upright into it. I expressed doubt that it ever got cold enough to light a fireplace. Aunt Marian agreed, but said it was part of the original house, which had been shipped from San Francisco a century ago.

I wanted to ask more about that, but K entered from the far room, pushing Tess in her wheelchair. Her eyes caught mine with a question and I answered with a reassuring smile.

"We'll have tea on the kitchen lanai, K," Marian said. "Wheel my sister there. Then take my grandniece's bags up to her room."

K nodded, glanced at me with dark, curious eyes, and

then left, pushing Tess back the way he'd come. Aunt Marian and I followed. The furniture was antique, very massive and dark in color and doubtlessly very valuable. Nothing I'd seen on the Mainland would compare with it.

When we were seated in the screened-in back porch (which both my aunts called a "lanai") and Tutu had retired, leaving us with iced tea in tall glasses, Aunt Marian turned to me.

"Meganne, I am surprised how you've grown. How tall are you now?"

"Five-nine. It seemed for a while I'd never stop growing, but I haven't gained an inch in two years."

I tried to make everything casual, but the mounting sense of something wrong was pressing in upon me. I wanted to get directly to the reasons I'd come there, but I knew Aunt Marian wouldn't answer my questions until she was finished with her own.

"I see. Rather pretty, too, with your mother's blue eyes and dark hair."

"Thank you." I looked toward Tess.

She said, "We were sorry to hear about your mother's death, Meganne. We didn't see our niece often, but she was a good woman."

"Very opinionated, however," Marian said curtly. "She no doubt inherited that from my other sister."

The crisp, brief remark brought back memories of my childhood when Aunt Marian and Aunt Tess had visited my mother, Margaret, and her mother, who was Marian's and Tess's youngest sister. The visit had been a nightmare of family arguments between my grandmother and Marian. I was too young to remember the details, but hearing Aunt Marian's flat statements triggered the pain of those old wounds.

Tess said quickly, "Tell us about your mother's death, Meganne."

"I wrote you about most of it."

"I know," Tess said, reaching out and taking my hand, "but there must have been details you didn't put in the letter."

I glanced sharply at the old woman. She smiled reassuringly, and I recognized that she was giving me the opportunity to say why I'd come.

Aunt Marian lowered her iced tea glass and nodded. "My sister is right, Meganne. Tell us."

I began slowly, recounting the events that I'd covered in the letter announcing my mother's death. She had not really seemed too ill at first. But the doctors had been unable to find a cause for her continued illness. The tests had shown little, yet my mother had slowly slipped away.

Marian nodded. "What was the official cause of death?"

"Some obscure blood disease. I have the medical term written down in some papers packed with my bags. I'll find it for you."

Aunt Marian waved the offer away. "No need for that. She's dead; that's the important issue."

She was so blunt I felt myself heating up inside. "No," I said firmly, "that's *not* the important issue."

"Oh?" Marian's eyebrows rose questioningly behind her glasses.

"My mother suffered more from the rumors about her than from her physical illness."

"What kind of rumors?" Marian's eyes brightened. She set her iced tea down and looked intently at me.

"Perhaps now's not the time to talk about such things, Marian," Tess warned. "Dear Meganne's had a long hard trip—."

"That's really why you came here, isn't it, Meganne?" Marian asked.

"Partly. At various times while I was growing up, I'd hear terrible stories about my mother being—possessed."

"Possessed, Meganne? You don't believe in such things, do you?"

"Not in this day and age. No."

"Yet such things are in the Bible, aren't they?"

I hesitated. How could I say that I had once made a public confession of faith in Jesus Christ as my Lord and Savior, but I now had trouble accepting everything in the New Testament as literally true? I wasn't at all sure I could explain my present feelings to Aunt Tess, who had always seemed to be a fine Christian, and her sister, whose rare letters always contained reference to her own belief in God.

"I don't know what I believe about demonism in the Bible, Aunt Marian. But I do know that I don't believe my mother was possessed. It was the rumors that hurt her. No matter where we went, and no matter how broad-minded and intelligent most people were, there were always some who repeated them."

"Your mother behaved strangely at times, didn't she?" Aunt Marian said tersely.

I swallowed, trying to calm the deep emotions that surged inside me. "My mother was not mentally ill, if that's what you mean."

Marian persisted. "But she did act peculiarly at times."

I didn't answer that. My mother had been a woman of intense emotions. She had always been excitable, but I always suspected that some old grievance had continually gnawed at her, making her the way she was.

"My mother was the victim of some terrible lies, and she was powerless to stop them, or to defend herself," I finally responded.

"What about her church friends, Meganne?"

I looked at Aunt Marian, feeling that she was deliberately pricking me with casually pointed questions. "She belonged to a church that believed in such things as possession and witchcraft."

"And you? Did you join that church?"

I shook my head. "I didn't join mother's church. When I got old enough to make my own decisions, I left her church and joined another."

"A liberal one, no doubt?"

"By some standards, yes; but one that practiced the love of God among its members."

"I see." Aunt Marian's thin lips tightened disapprovingly. And yet there seemed to be something about her eyes that showed a certain satisfaction. It was as though she was sure all along that I was misguided in my spiritual life and she had just confirmed it.

I was tired of her questioning. Seeing as she had not masked her dislike of my mother, I decided to be equally frank with her. "I'd like to know the truth about my mother's mother—my Grandmother Rogers—and why she left this house before my mother was born and never returned," I said looking directly at Aunt Marian. "I'd like to know what terrible things happened, which still were there years later, to ruin my mother's life."

"You believe you can overcome such things, Meganne?"

"Yes, Marian, I do."

"You may call me *Aunt* Marian!"

It came as a slap. It was as though I were a little girl again, and my visiting great-aunt was reprimanding me with a firm determination to keep me in my place. This sharp old lady would obviously reveal nothing; I would have to search for my answers elsewhere.

"If you'll excuse me," I said, rising abruptly, "I'm very tired."

Aunt Marian seemed amused. "Of course. Tutu will show you to your room."

Tess spoke up. "Meganne, my dear, if you'll push my chair to the foot of the stairs—."

"Oh, sister!" Marian protested. "I'm sure Meganne's

much too exhausted to delay her retiring a moment longer." Aunt Marian raised her voice. "Tutu!"

The big Hawaiian woman appeared in the doorway, listened briefly to her employer's instructions, and then led
me back into the dreary old mansion and up the stairs.

I stumbled after her, my mind reeling, wondering what I
had gotten myself into.

Chapter Three

Tutu heaved her great bulk up the banistered, deeply carpeted stairs with such effort I was alarmed for her heart. She laughed and assured me she was all right. She'd been climbing those stairs for many years and expected to do so for many more.

She led me past the second story, pointing out Aunt Marian's and Aunt Tess's "chambers"—as Tutu called them—with the bathroom at the end of the hall. Tutu said she slept near the bathroom, close to the older women.

"But only until we get a new nurse," Tutu puffed, starting up a third, narrower flight of stairs. "Then I'll go back to sleeping in the little house out back, with my husband."

"Tutu, did you know my mother?"

She shook her big head so the jowls jiggled. "No, I never saw her. Nor her mother, either."

I silently followed her down a musty, dim hallway that echoed with our footsteps. The old floors squeaked as we walked. There was a foreboding sense of gloom. I glanced around nervously, peering over my shoulder, but Tutu didn't seem to notice. She opened a room in the far end of the third-story hallway and switched on a light.

"K brought your bags up," Tutu said, waving a big arm at the familiar items. "I'll help you unpack and get settled."

"No, thank you, Tutu; that's not necessary. I'll do it tomorrow. Tonight I think I'll just turn in. Jet-lag is catching up to me, I guess."

The big Hawaiian woman nodded. As she showed me around the room I realized that this was a gable in the strange conglomeration of upper rooms. She said I would use the downstairs bathroom, the one on the second floor by my great-aunts' chambers.

I thanked Tutu and closed the door. By the light of an antique wall bracket, I could see the small living quarters allotted to me. The draperies were heavy and old, smelling of dust and disuse. I pulled them open and was pleased to see a whole wall of sliding glass doors, with louvered sections on each side.

I found the locking mechanism and opened the door. A rusted screen blocked entrance to a tiny balcony faintly visible from the small light behind me. I started to slide the screen open, but drew back with a gasp of surprise.

A lizard clung to the outside, his tiny feet gripping the holes in the screen. I backed up involuntarily. Then I forced a little chuckle. A gecko. I'd read about them someplace in my preparation for the island visit. Opaque, almost transparent, they were harmless insect eaters. Still, I wasn't fond of any cold-blooded creature. I turned back into the room and completed my inspection.

"Spooky," I said aloud, confirming what my mind had been telling me.

But it was more than that. There was a heaviness about the place, a feeling more than a tangible thing. Maybe it was the *kona*, I thought. The air was totally dead and still. I couldn't hear the trees swaying or the palm fronds rattling.

There was an intense blackness, which seemed to swallow up everything beyond the little balcony railing.

In the distance, a flash of sheet lightning momentarily lit up the sky. I glimpsed great trees and a precipice. Was this where Aunt Tess's practical nurse had fallen to her death? If so, that meant the ocean must be just beyond the encircling stand of trees. I strained to hear the surf, but not a sound came out of the night.

I shivered and turned to unpacking. Tess had urged me not to stay, but I'd have to remain until I earned enough money to return to the Mainland. And I didn't intend to do that until I had the answers that had brought me here.

Inside a musty closet I saw a sweater hanging on a wide wooden hanger. I pushed it aside to make room for my few belongings.

The garment collapsed, striking the carpeted floor.

I reached for the hanger. It was gone. It had simply turned to dust at my touch. Uncertainly, I picked up the old sweater. There were tiny holes in the shoulder.

"Termites!" I said softly. "It has to be termites. They ate everything except the shell of the hanger, and when I touched it—."

I realized that it was possible for someone to lean against a seemingly solid wooden railing and not know it was totally eaten away inside. But Alema sounded like a Hawaiian name. Would a local woman, reared on the Islands, have made such a fatal error?

I found myself becoming increasingly involved emotionally in something I couldn't understand.

But why? I could see no visible danger to myself, or any reason why aunts I hardly knew would harm me.

I walked over to a beautiful old table with elaborately carved legs and a heavy marble top. I pushed aside the open Bible that lay there and began to place my cosmetics on the marbled top.

My eyes were drawn to the Bible where a verse had been marked in bright yellow see-through ink. Idly, I leaned closer to read the words.

"For we wrestle not against flesh and blood, but against principalities, against powers, against the rulers of the darkness of this world, against spiritual wickedness in high places."

Paul's words in Ephesians 6:12 were familiar to me. I'd read them often enough before I'd given up reading the Bible and praying, things that once were daily parts of my life. But somehow, at this moment, the verse seemed different—as though it were a warning.

Meganne Fields, I told myself firmly, *you're starting to let your imagination run away with you. Now stop it!*

But the mystery of this old house had unlocked a dark closet of my mind and thoughts that I'd tried to dismiss for years. Was it possible, I asked myself, that my mother did have something dark and sinister inside? Had I been infected with the same thing? Was I, somehow, as someone had once said of my mother, 'the devil's child?'

Two young men I had loved had thought such rumors might be possible: one when I was only seventeen, and just recently a young man I was engaged to marry. Instead of telling me frankly that he was afraid of my "heritage," he had claimed that we were not "suited" to one another. "Too different in our likes and dislikes." But his sister had later revealed that he had heard too many rumors and was uncomfortable with the prospects of our life together.

I forced such thoughts from my mind and turned to finish my unpacking. Yet I couldn't shake the feeling that somehow I had stumbled into something shadowy but real, something tragic and evil. In fact, the thought crossed my mind that my appearance had somehow been the precipitating event, which was going to bring some unholy cauldron of terror to a boil.

I stepped to the screen door and placed my cupped hands against my temples, shading my eyes. It was still very quiet out there. A distant flash of lightning momentarily touched the tall trees. But there was nothing else, no sound, no breeze—just this oppressive sense of forboding.

Trying to shake that feeling, I impulsively slid the screen door open after making sure the little gecko lizard was gone. I stepped out into the night and moved cautiously onto the little balcony. The boards under my feet seemed solid enough. I eased across to the edge. My fingers felt a fancy wrought-iron railing, which came up to my waist. I pushed on it. Solid. No danger there.

I leaned cautiously against the railing and cocked my head to listen to the night. At first, it seemed as deathly still as before. Then I caught a faint noise that sounded like a freight train was passing at a great distance; yet the sound continued, never really fading into the distance. Surf, I thought. It had to be just beyond that line of trees and straight down. But it was reassuring to know something was normal out there in that hushed, brooding night.

With a sigh, I turned back to the room. I slid the screen door shut and started to do the same with the heavy glass door. But I was on the third story, facing the ocean. No vines climbed up this far. There was no danger from intruders, so I left the glass door open. If the trade winds came back, they'd blow coolly across my bed.

I stepped into the closet and began undressing. I took off the leis that had been presented by K at the airport. I looked around for some place to hang them where I could still see and smell them and chose the high wooden post of the headboard. Hadn't I read someplace that it was considered good luck to hang the first flower lei you got over your bedpost?

My eyes fell again on the open Bible and its somehow disturbing words: "For we wrestle not against flesh and blood. . . ." I closed it quickly and started back into the closet. Then I stopped. I reached down and casually flipped the pages open again. Psalms. That was good. There was comfort in many of King David's beautifully written songs.

Someone had marked a verse, very lightly, with faded pencil. I bent forward to read. "And call upon me in the day of trouble: I will deliver thee, and thou shalt glorify me."

That was nice, even if I didn't really believe it. I left the page open to Psalm 50, undressed, removed my makeup, and put on my gown. It was so hot that I wouldn't even need the sheet so I turned it down and slid into the bed forgetting to turn off the light.

As I started to get up to turn it off, my eyes went to the ceiling. The frescoes were graceful and sweeping, with long pleasant lines radiating out from the corners to intertwine in the center.

But in the middle of those beautiful lines there was a hideous face of molded plaster. I didn't know if it represented a demon or gargoyle, but I'd seen enough Victorian houses in San Francisco to know such things were part of the decor.

Yet I'd never seen one quite like this. A single horn extended from the center of the imaginative forehead. The ears were pointed and elongated. The nose was thin and high above a leering mouth.

But it was the eyes that held my gaze. They were dark, almost black, and seemed to reflect the light from the small electric fixture. They seemed to follow me as I got up and walked toward the light switch. Whoever the artist had been, he'd done a good job of creating an illusion of life in this representation of something inhuman.

I forced myself to snap off the light and return to the bed. The oppressive stillness of the night began to seep over me. It was all in my head, I knew, and I was strong enough to make my mind dismiss the strange creation.

I let my body relax and slipped into a troubled sleep. I wasn't sure if I dreamed it, or if I really heard distant quarreling. But that impression was lost in a slow roll of thunder that gradually approached. Suddenly, a loud crash jerked me upright in the bed.

The sky was lighted with frequent flashes. The thunder boomed about me. Then the rain came. It was harder than anything I'd ever seen, as though a streak of lightning had ripped the dark underside of the clouds and all the water in the sky was being dumped out at once.

Well, I told myself, the storm had broken. Tomorrow it would be clear again, the trade winds would return, and the world would be beautiful. I went back to sleep with the storm rumbling about the old mansion called Hale Aloha.

Chapter Four

I awoke to the sound of little Japanese doves outside my sliding screen door. I raised myself on one elbow and looked out. The sun was high and bright. The trade winds were blowing gently through the screen and across my bed, stirring the fragrance of the flowers in my leis.

I jumped out of bed and stepped to the screen. The shadows and fears of the night were gone. I glanced at the ceiling. The demon's head was simply plaster, nothing more. I remembered something I'd heard long ago about witchcraft and demonism when my father, a small town newspaper editor, was working on a case that was supposed to involve black magic. Once the truth was known, dad had written, "All magic, witchcraft and other such things exist in the imagination alone."

The sea was visible off to my right in a place where the cliff dipped. The water was a magnificent blue green, stretching out endlessly to round off into nothingness at the horizon. Some beautiful cumulous clouds were riding the bluest sky I'd ever seen. The sun, slanting through the dense trees at the cliff's edge, warmed my face.

Impulsively, I rushed to the closet and grabbed my one-piece, aqua bathing suit. I was sure my aunts wouldn't mind if I took a quick dip before breakfast. Well, I wasn't quite sure about Aunt Marian, but I ignored that thought. I ran down the stairs to the second floor, brushed my teeth in the bathroom, grabbed a towel off one of the heavy wooden racks, and headed toward the landing above the first floor.

For a moment, I was tempted to slide down the huge old banisters to the living room below. But I resisted and hurried down the deeply carpeted stairs and found my way into the breakfast room.

"Ah, my dear," Tess greeted me from her wheelchair. "There you are!"

Aunt Marian turned from pouring some pinkish juice into a small glass. "We wondered if you were going to sleep all day. I'm sure you don't mind that we had breakfast without you?"

I wasn't quite sure how she meant that, but I was feeling too happy to let it bother me. "I'm going to take a quick swim before breakfast. I'm not hungry, anyway."

I started to run out but Tess stopped me. "Meganne, dear, would you mind pushing me outside where I can enjoy the sunshine?"

There seemed to be an underlying hint of something in her words. I threw my towel over my shoulder and began pushing the chair toward the outside door.

"Really, sister," Aunt Marian said with some feeling, "you shouldn't expect your niece to do that. K is just outside; I'll call him to help you."

I protested, "Oh, I don't mind!"

Aunt Marian's voice was firm. "Nonsense, Meganne! Just leave the chair where it is."

I stopped and looked at Aunt Marian. There was a bright color to her cheeks and her eyes seemed to snap. I glanced at Tess. She turned her head to quietly look up over her shoulder at me.

"It's all right, Meganne dear," she said quietly. "You run along. But be careful."

I shrugged and hurried outside. But the joy of the day had somehow been scarred. It was like a shadow from a passing cloud weakening the sun's power. And yet it was more than that, too. It seemed Aunt Marian was deliberately trying to keep me from being alone with her sister.

"Ho!" I recognized K's exclamation. He was dressed in zori sandals, cutoff blue jeans, and a somewhat tattered white T-shirt. He backed out of a hedge where he'd been using a heavy pair of clippers. "Ho! You think da *kine* surf up?"

I blinked, then smiled. He was teasing me. I noticed that his voice tended to remain high at the end of a sentence. It was a trait I'd also detected in Tutu's speech.

"Which way to the beach, K?"

"You going swim alone, huh?"

"I'll be careful!"

"Never swim alone; old Hawaiian rule."

"Old Mainland rule, too," I laughed. "But I'm a good swimmer and I'm not afraid. Besides, Aunt Marian wants you inside. Which way down this cliff to the beach?"

He pointed with the shears. "Trail very steep. Mainland *haole wahine* be planty careful, heh?"

I wondered if he lapsed into pidgin English when he was excited. But it didn't matter. I ran along the way he'd pointed. Once I stopped in surprise and bent over. Orchids! Hundreds of them. Growing wild. Oh, what a beautiful place! I ran to the edge of the forest, pricked myself on a scraggly tree, and immediately gained more respect for the possible dangers even in paradise.

I half-ran, half-slid down the steep volcanic trail, scraping my palms a couple times from reaching out to support myself. But I learned. *Careful, Meganne! Take your time!*

I ran across the little stretch of sand, feeling the warm particles squish under my tennis shoes. I stopped, yanked them off, and ran on. Some transparent blue things were scattered on the sand. They reminded me of seaweed particles on California's beaches. I used to step on them to hear them pop. But this time I was anxious to get into the welcoming white surf with its blue green swells beyond. I dropped my towel and plunged into the waves.

They were wonderful! Warmer than California's waters, swelling gently to tall rolls that sped toward the white sandy beach to explode in glorious plumes of foaming surf.

"Hey! Hey!"

I heard the male voice as I came up out of the waves. He was dressed in white tennis shoes and faded blue print bathing trunks. He was taller than K. This deeply-tanned, well-muscled man was probably in his early thirties. He had a small reddish moustache although his hair was wavy brown. There was something about his craggy features that was strangely handsome.

He cupped his hands to his mouth and called to me.

I stood up in the chest high water and frowned. "What?" I called over the sound of the surf.

"Come out!"

I couldn't believe the words. Who was he to be ordering me out of the sea? I knew this beach was part of my aunts' property, because I was directly below the cliff and could see part of one high chimney rising above the trees. I turned my back on the stranger and did a neat surface dive into an incoming wave.

Pain hit me like an electric shock. It was so sudden and severe I involuntarily inhaled. A mouthful of sea water gagged me. I wanted to scream with the intensity of the unexplained pain that shot through my shoulders, back, and rib cage. I tried to see what was attacking me, but couldn't see anything. Whatever it was apparently was invisible in the water, or had stung me in many places at once and then fallen into the sea.

Sobbing, gagging, and swallowing salt water, I staggered through the surf toward the beach. The pain was so great I doubled over and fell to my knees.

The waves rushed from behind, lifted me, and carried me forward a few feet. I was frantically trying to find the cause of the pain when I felt myself lifted again.

But this time it wasn't the waves. The stranger was carrying me toward the white sand beach. I heard gruff, commanding words but I hurt too much to understand.

He put me down hard on the beach at the water's edge and ran toward the black cliff. I wanted to cry out, "Don't leave me!" but the words were distorted by the sobbing, moaning sounds in my throat.

The stranger was back in a moment. I tore my frightened gaze from the ugly red welts appearing on my shoulders and arms and caught a whiff of ammonia.

"This'll help take the pain out," he said, pouring the liquid liberally into his cupped left palm. "It's ammonia, but it'll hurt less than the stings."

He applied it quickly to my shoulders. I instinctively drew away from his touch. He seemed to understand and thrust the bottle into my wet hands. "Here. Do your arms."

My hands were trembling so hard with the severity of the pain that I spilled much of the ammonia on the sand. But as I splashed the liquid onto my bare skin, I felt the pain start to ease a little.

When I could finally control my frantic applications, I took a shuddering breath and tried to stand. I was surprised to find how weak-kneed I felt. I staggered and his hands caught me.

"Than . . . thanks!" I finally managed to gasp. "What happened?"

"Portuguese man-of-war! Didn't you see them?"

I shook my head. "I didn't see anything. I was just swimming along when something started hurting me so much it felt like electric shocks. It was so bad I couldn't breathe."

"You should have seen them on the beach, miss. All washed up from last night's storm."

"You mean those transparent blue things with the long string? I thought they were some kind of seaweed."

He shook his head. "Living creatures. They sting like nothing else in this world! And can be quite dangerous."

I looked at my red-lashed skin. The exterior pain was lessening, but now it seemed to go deeper, penetrating into the shoulder blades and my elbow sockets. "You sure it was nothing more than those little blue things?"

He managed a soft chuckle. "I'm sure. But those little blue things, as you call them, are going to make you miserable for some time, even with the ammonia, although it helps. That's why I always keep some close by when I come down here."

I was suddenly aware that I was a mess. My hair was tangled with streaming rivulets of sea water. My eyes were undoubtedly blurred and red from the pain and shock. My extremely white bare legs were in sharp contrast to the angry red welts and some ugly black and blue marks beginning to form.

"You're a Mainland *haole*, aren't you, miss?"

"I beg your pardon?"

"I mean, you just flew in from the Mainland. Right?"

"Last night."

"May I ask what you're doing here?"

I looked up sharply, hurting enough that I was about to say it wasn't any of his business, but he read my mind. He held up brown hands. "I mean, what're you doing swimming alone in this out-of-the-way place?"

"I'm staying with relatives close by."

"Well, in case you stay awhile, maybe we should introduce ourselves? I'm Jim Starrett."

"Meganne Fields." I started to shake hands, but the pain in my arm stopped me.

"You better sit down and rest awhile, Miss Fields," he said. He took my hand gingerly and helped me ease down to my knees. I felt very uncomfortable about my appearance, but I was flattered that he seemed genuinely interested.

"How'd you find this place?"

"I saw the beach from up on the cliff and asked a man there how to get down here."

Jim frowned. "All kinds of dangers around here, Miss Fields."

"Call me Meganne."

"All kinds of dangers around here, Meganne," he repeated. "Like the Portuguese man-of-war."

I managed a smile and shook my hair out of my face, running my fingers through the long strands to smooth them. "I'm beginning to find that out. Is there anything else I should be careful of?"

"I guess you know about the danger of putting a blade of grass in your mouth?"

"Why on earth is that dangerous?"

"Liver flukes."

"I never heard of them."

"They don't put that in the visitors' brochures, but these giant African snails—you seen them?"

I shook my head.

"Six inches long, and pretty as any snail shell you'll ever see. Harmless themselves, but part of their unfortunate life cycle is to carry liver parasites. The snails leave the fluke's eggs on the grass. You put the grass in your mouth and your body becomes host to those—"

"Mr. Starrett, if you're . . ."

"My name is Jim. Please call me that."

"Jim, if you're trying to scare me, you're succeeding."

"Don't mean to scare you, but you should be warned. I'm surprised your relatives didn't tell you about dangers like that."

"Well, to be honest, I didn't give them much chance."

"You didn't tell me who your relatives are, Meganne."

"My aunts. Well, great-aunts. They live in that old Victorian mansion on top of the hill."

"Those two old ladies?" He jerked a thumb over his shoulder toward the black cliff. "You're related to them?"

"They're my last living relatives. You know them?"

Jim's face clouded. The friendly, open conversation seemed to have been stifled as suddenly as water dumped on a small flame douses it.

"You'd better be getting back to them," he said. Suddenly he seemed mysteriously aloof; or perhaps it was a sudden loss of interest.

He reached out a hand and pulled me to my feet. "You think you can climb that steep trail now?"

I found myself drawing into my own protective shell. The mention of my aunts and the old house had cleanly sliced our prospective friendship. "I can manage, thank you."

We walked toward the cliff. I found him attractive in spite of the sullen moroseness which seemed to have settled over him and driven our conversation into a knothole. I wondered if he was the type of man to be easily scared off by the strange circumstances that surrounded me.

We came to the foot of the cliff. Jim asked, "You sure you can make it?"

"I'm sure. Thanks for the help."

"It's nothing. Well, aloha, Meganne Fields."

He turned to the right and began climbing the narrow trail away from Hale Aloha. He was quickly lost to sight in the brush that gripped the black rocks.

I climbed to the left, away from Jim Starrett, wondering if the tears in my eyes were from the pain of the Portuguese man-of-war or from a feeling of rejection.

Chapter Five

I reached the top of the cliff and held onto some vines to catch my breath. K was talking to a beautiful black-haired girl at an opening between the high oleanders, which obviously marked one end of my aunts' property. She was tiny, barely over five feet tall, but perfect in form and face, her figure accented by a bright orange bikini.

K caught sight of me and dropped his pruning shears. He said something to the girl, then ran toward me.

"You all right? What happened?"

"I'm all right," I puffed, still recovering my breath from the climb. "I lost an encounter with a Portuguese man-of-war."

"Ho! You look like somebody used a whip on you!"

"It's all right, K." I lowered my voice. "Who's she?"

"Her? Malia, adopted daughter of Tutu Kamala."

"She's . . . beautiful, isn't she?"

"Ho! You got good eyes, sistah!"

"Is she Hawaiian?" I found myself fascinated with this tiny but perfectly lovely girl.

"She's pure and simple cosmopolitan."

"What's that?"

"Ho! All the *kine* mix up blood: Hawaiian, Chinese, Japanese, Portuguese, maybe little Filippino, and *haole*. Lots island girls like her!" His bantering voice lowered instantly. "You watch out for dat sistah, Miss Fields, you bet!"

I looked questioningly into K's brown eyes, but they were hooded and shadowed. He turned abruptly and led me to the one he'd called Malia. Up close, I could see her skin was not brown or yellow, but a golden, creamy hue without a flaw of any kind. I suddenly felt very untidy and self-conscious.

Malia's dark eyes were wide and clear. I could see her as the star of some epic South Sea island movie. She smiled at me in greeting, but didn't offer to shake hands. Neither did I.

"Welcome to our island, Meganne," she said in a voice so low and melodious I was startled. "Tutu has told me about you, and K was speaking of you just a few minutes ago."

"It's good to meet you, Malia."

We chatted briefly about my encounter with the man-of-war, then I excused myself, and walked on toward Hale Aloha, standing in the open grassy area between great rings of tall rain forest trees, which seemed to respectfully circle the old house as though somehow afraid to come too close.

I hoped to avoid my aunts, especially Marian, in my present condition. My skin still stung from the attack I'd suffered in the water, and I ached deep down inside.

I slipped up the stairs to the bathroom, thinking about the people I'd met. Why had Jim Starrett suddenly seemed distant and aloof when he'd found out who I was? I was also curious about Malia. What had prompted K to whisper a warning about her?

I showered, wrapped myself in a towel, and went to my room on the third floor. I was surprised when I opened the door to see that it was dark. A glance at the screened balcony told me why; the sun had gone behind a huge cloud. It bothered me, somehow, so I walked to the screen, slid it open, and stepped outside to take a better look at the sky.

Thunk! Something thudded softly into the door jamb beside my head. Instinctively I ducked and leaped back inside the bedroom. What in the world was that? I wondered.

I eased forward again, holding the towel tightly about myself, and craned my neck to where I could see onto the balcony.

An arrow stuck in the wood. The feathered shaft was still reverberating.

A glance at the grounds below showed no one in sight. I guessed the arrow had come from the tall, shadowy line of rain forest trees by the cliff's edge. But was it an accident? It had to be. Nobody had any reason to shoot at me! And an arrow? Here, in Hawaii?

I stood inside the room, shivering from the pain of the stings, the uncertainty of what had just happened, and the problem of what to do about it. Would I alarm my aunts if I told them?

I slipped into the closet, dressed quickly, and started out of the room. Then, on an impulse, I stepped to the screen door, which still stood slightly open. I took a deep breath and reached around the sheltering side of the door jamb, feeling for the arrow.

My fingers touched rough wooden planks and peeling paint, but no arrow shaft. I swung my hand in a wider arc, feeling uselessly for the thing I knew was there.

But it wasn't.

I peered around the corner of the open door, half-convinced I was making a fool of myself, and saw that the arrow was gone. There was a fresh penetration mark in the wood, but that was all.

I backed into the room and sat down heavily on the bed. Had I imagined it? Had my mind started playing tricks on me? Three stories up, no ladder or vines or any way to climb the side of that house, and yet the arrow was gone.

If there had been one.

The sun, instead of overpowering the clouds that had darkened it a few minutes ago, remained hidden. The sense of impending doom from an unknown adversary oozed over me like a heavy blanket. Whether that arrow was real or not, the feeling of fear that seeped over me was.

I got dressed and went downstairs.

Aunt Marian saw me first. She sat at a huge dining table with heavy old-fashioned chairs. "What happened to you?" Aunt Marian demanded. She put down her Bible and came toward me.

"Portuguese Man-of-War," I explained. "I look a fright."

Tess wheeled her chair closer to me. "Are you all right?"

"I'm all right, thanks. But I've had quite a scare."

"Sit down and tell us about it," Aunt Marian said.

I told about the stinging attack and the meeting with Jim Starrett and Malia. But I didn't mention the arrow. The other incidents and people were obviously provable, but I wasn't completely sure, even now, that I'd actually seen that arrow narrowly miss me.

"You might have drowned, you know." Aunt Marian said.

"I know. I won't swim alone any more."

I wanted to get Aunt Tess alone, but there didn't seem to be any discreet way to suggest that. Instead I'd have to take a more direct route by asking questions with both of them present.

"Aunt Marian," I said. "What does Jim Starrett do?"

"I don't know, really. He's a strange one."

"How so?"

Aunt Marian shrugged, peering at me over the top of her dark-rimmed glasses. "Nobody really knows where he came from, or what he does. He lives alone in that house beyond the oleander hedge. Been there about a year now, maybe a little less. Frankly, Meganne, I'd advise you to avoid him."

I looked at Aunt Tess. She was looking at me with concern but saying nothing.

"Does K work for you full time?"

"Why, yes, for years. He's a local man. Good worker. Does all kinds of things around the place."

Thinking I was curious about the members of the household staff, Aunt Marian began describing their backgrounds to me. When she mentioned Tutu, I asked, "Is Malia really Tutu's adopted daughter?"

"Hawaiian adoption, Meganne. In the old days, it was common for a Hawaiian family to give a child to someone else," Aunt Marian answered.

"You're saying that Tutu didn't legally adopt Malia?"

"No need to. Tutu's heart is as big as her body. She found this beautiful girl some years ago, learned she was orphaned and had been living like a wild dog in the rain forest. So Tutu adopted her."

"You don't really know her background then?"

Aunt Marian snorted. "What's there to know? She was there and Tutu took her in. That's the old Hawaiian way."

I started to ask another question, but spotted a warning look in Tess's eyes. Even so I decided to risk one more question.

"Do any of the men around here hunt?"

"Hunt? Of course not! . . . Really, Meganne! Your questions are ridiculous." She turned toward Tess with a look of exasperation and then glanced back at me in a gesture of dismissal.

"You'd probably better run down to Tutu's house and have her take a look at those stings, even though this is her day off."

Before I could reply, Aunt Marian arose and walked out of the room.

I felt the old hurts open deep inside me. I guess the pain showed. Tess reached a thin, blue-veined hand from her lap and pulled me close to her wheelchair.

"Don't mind her, Meganne, my dear."

"She treats me just as she did when I was a little girl!"

I glanced up, making sure Aunt Marian wasn't close enough to hear me. "Aunt Tess, you said something that concerns me. . . ."

"Not now, dear!"

"Aunt Marian's down at the far end of the other room," I assured her. "I can see her from here. Now, please tell me what's going on?"

Tess's voice dropped to a whisper as she turned in her wheelchair so she could also see her sister. "I can't tell you, Meganne, because I don't really know. But you're in danger every minute you stay under this roof!"

"In danger? From whom?"

"I don't know! But when Alema went through that railing, I knew . . . She's coming back!" Tess raised her voice casually so it would carry to her sister. "I'm sure you'll find Tutu's home remedies will greatly ease your distress, Meganne."

I stood quickly. "I'm sure I will."

Aunt Marian stopped abruptly and turned back the way she'd come. Tess watched her sister, and then turned to me. "Meganne, I've prayed for you daily since you were a little girl; do you know that?"

"No, but I'm not surprised. Did you pray for my happiness?"

"Of course! And much more, Meganne!"

"Well, I haven't had much happiness so far; I can tell you that."

"It'll come, Meganne. It'll come! God's promises are true, and I've claimed them for you to have a happy, wonderful life."

"So far, Aunt Tess, your prayers about that are unanswered. In fact . . ."

When I hesitated, Tess guessed the truth. "So you're mad at God, are you?"

"Something like that," I confessed.

"I'll pray about that, too, Meganne. . . . You'd better go now."

I took a quick step backward out of Aunt Marian's line of sight and eased out the door and into the yard, nearly stumbling over two cats—one solid white, the other black—which suddenly shot out from under me and vanished into the shelter of a pandanus at the corner of the house.

"Ho!" K's customary exclamation had a light touch to it. "They scare you, huh?"

"I didn't see them at first. Yes, they frightened me."

"No need. They're just a couple of wild house cats that come down from the mountains to eat the food we set out for them." He turned back to his hedge trimming, and I went on toward Tutu's house, which was barely visible in the dense undergrowth at the far right side of Hale Aloha.

I glanced at the sky. Fast-moving clouds had totally swallowed the sun. The smell of distant rain, born on the trade winds, came faintly to my nose. I walked on toward Tutu's house, wondering if someone was behind the line of trees or a hedge somewhere with a bow and arrow in hand.

Or had I imagined the whole thing?

I still wasn't sure, and that was bad. I was having a hard enough time hanging onto my emotions and mental faculties without doubting what I'd seen with my own eyes.

I began to hurry, for there was something in the air suggesting the same sense of lurking evil that had intimidated me last night. Whatever it was, I sensed it watching me as I reached Tutu's house, walked up on the sagging wooden porch, and knocked at the door, which was protected only by a rusted screen full of holes.

Chapter Six

The house was small, of single-wall construction painted dark green. A rusted corrugated tin roof showed signs of great age, but the drabness of the house at the edge of the rain forest was brightened by a profusion of wild flowers and plants, which graced the window boxes and lined the short stilt foundation.

My knock was answered by ponderous bare feet slapping on wooden flooring. Tutu's enormous bulk darkened the door screen.

"*Auwe! Ke aha keia?*" Her motherly concern took in my stings at a glance. Tutu threw open the screen door and ushered me into the dark, cool room. She motioned me to a chair, opened my blouse, and began examining my stings with gentle hands.

"You get stung planty, huh?" Tutu didn't want an answer. She was just making conversation. "Hurt planty, yes?"

I nodded. Lots of white blisters like mosquito welts were covering my arms, shoulders, back, and rib cage. An angry blue and red color was spreading over the right shoulder.

"Ammonia?" Tutu asked.

"Yes."

"Who?"

"Jim Starrett. He put ammonia on right after it happened."

"Good!" Tutu finished her examination and motioned for me to replace my blouse. "Pain go 'way hapa-hour— maybeso more, maybeso less! You have *kaukau?*" She made eating motions.

"I haven't had breakfast," I admitted.

"Papaya! I show you." Tutu heaved her enormous bulk into action. She padded to the old refrigerator and removed a pumpkin-colored fruit about the size of a cantaloupe. She sliced it in half, placed the larger section before me, and pressed a spoon into my hand. I sat down at the Formica-topped table and took a tentative bite.

"Why, Tutu! This is delicious! Thank you!"

"Now try guava juice." Tutu poured some pinkish thick liquid into a small glass and set it before me. *"Kaukau,"* she announced with the air of authority assumed by people who know such things. "Make pain go 'way!"

A male voice hailed from outside. "Tutu! You home?"

"Derek!" Tutu cried, turning away to throw open the screen door. "Come in! Come in!"

He was not quite six feet tall, very blond, with gold wire-framed glasses setting above some kind of white salve he'd put on the end of his sunburned nose. The eyeglass lenses were so large I knew they had to be plastic, because real glass would have weighed too much for his nose.

Tutu engulfed the man in her big arms. *"Hele mai! Awi-wi!"* she cried.

He caught sight of me and disengaged Tutu's huge arms. "Hello! What have we here?"

"Derek," Tutu said with a flourish of her huge arms in my

direction, "this here is Meganne Fields, grandniece of Marian and Tess."

Derek smiled from his sunburned face. "Don't tell me! You're a pretty mainland *wahine* who just got in! I can tell because you're not all burned to a crisp!"

"Flew in last night," I said, wiping my fingers on a white paper napkin Tutu had given me. I offered him my right hand. "From San Francisco."

"Hello, San Francisco!" Derek advanced across the room and took my fingers lightly in his right hand. He bent over them elaborately, swept off his native *kahala* hat, and kissed my fingers lightly. "Aloha, San Francisco!"

I felt the brush of a small moustache. He smiled, showing good teeth and pale blue eyes partially protected by heavy blond eyebrows. Then he caught sight of the angry welts on my arms.

"Hurt much?" he asked.

"It's easing."

Tutu beamed at him. He still held lightly to my fingers. His naturally blond hair was wavy and neatly combed, except around the ears where the quick removal of his hat had dislodged some almost-white hairs. Yet he didn't seem more than six to eight years older than I.

"Derek what?" I asked.

"Norton. But Derek's fine. What brings you to our remote part of this island?"

I tried to keep it light. "I might ask you the same thing. What do you do, Mr. Norton?"

"Derek," he corrected me with a wag of a forefinger. He turned to Tutu. "What do I do, Tutu?"

"Beach bum!" Tutu exploded the words and laughed. "But you treat this *wahine* right or you be food for moray eels! She got one da *kine* great-aunt!"

I noticed Tutu said "one" aunt, not two. Obviously Aunt Marian was not so special to his huge brown-skinned woman with the hearty hospitality.

"Hey, beach bum! Open da *kine* door! Husband come!"

Derek opened the screen door for the largest man I'd ever seen. He was a good foot taller than I, or about six-seven. I guessed he weighed at least three hundred and seventy-five pounds. His once-black curly hair was graying. His nose was enormous, and he was nearly beardless with large, friendly eyes.

"*Aloha kakahiaka*, Meganne!" he cried. We hadn't been introduced, but he obviously knew who I was. For all his bulk, he moved with the Hawaiian's natural grace. "*Pehea oe?*" he said, kissing me on both cheeks and then holding me at arm's length to look at me.

I looked helplessly at Tutu, but she was beaming so happily at her husband that Derek felt he should come to my rescue. "Kupuna says, 'Good morning! How are you?' "

"What'd you call him?" I asked.

"*Kupuna* is really 'grandparent' or 'ancestor.' But most of us call him Tutu Kane Makua. Literally, that means 'granny,' 'husband,' and finally, 'parent.' But he doesn't mind what you call him, do you Tutu Kane Makua?"

The huge Hawaiian grinned. "Friends are able to call me what they want, and I am happy."

I liked him and his wife very much. Derek also seemed warm and friendly. In fact, I thought, it seems everyone's nice around here except my Great-Aunt Marian—and the person who had used me for target practice.

"Meganne," Derek said, taking my hand and pulling me to my feet, "how about letting me show you around? Maybe teach you some Hawaiian words?"

Tutu spoke briefly. "Meganne stays here."

It surprised me to hear the note of finality in the Hawaiian woman's words. Derek glanced sharply at her, smiled, and then apologized.

"Of course! I should have realized! All those stings are so

painful! But perhaps another time?"

I smiled at him. "I'd like a rain check, please."

"One rain check coming up." Derek tore off a piece of my napkin and solemnly handed it to me. "Well, everybody, I've got to be going."

Tutu seemed miffed. "You no like da *kine* visit for me?"

Derek threw up his hands in mock surrender. "OK! OK! I'll stay."

The conversation never seemed to slacken. It was warm and friendly. We sat around and talked as though nobody had a care in the world. And, for a while, I didn't remember my reasons for coming to Hawaii, Tess's whispered warning, or the arrow that had come within inches of my face.

The huge Hawaiian explained that he was the son of a *kahuna*, an authentic Hawaiian priest who believed in the gods of old Hawaii. I had a feeling the older man was uncomfortable discussing his personal life. But his wife was so amiable that nobody seemed to notice when the graying man fell silent and the talk shifted naturally to her.

"What about yourself, Tutu? What's your background? Are you a high priestess or something?" I asked.

Her eyes sobered. I thought for a moment I'd offended her. The gray in her hair caught a stray shaft of sunlight when the clouds parted for a moment and a sunbeam poked through the house. Then the clouds closed in again. The Hawaiian woman spread her big, gentle hands and spoke softly, movingly, in a way the natives did.

"God went give me one piece land," she began. She opened her arms wide so that great masses of smooth flesh dangled. "I plant guava, pineapple. I plant taro for poi. I plant planty food for all my children and *moopunas*."

Derek whispered to me. "She means 'grandchildren.' "

Tutu continued. "I make my land green. Planty food, that's why." Tutu looked slowly at each of us. "Roof. Food.

Family. What else can I ask?"

We parted on that mellow thought. Derek said he would walk me over to Hale Aloha. We said our goodbyes and started across the open section between the little Hawaiian house and the mansion. The skies had turned dark. Rain obviously was coming soon.

"She has such a beautiful philosophy," I said.

Derek looked down at me and gingerly rubbed his sun-burned nose. "She doesn't own any land. She's rented this piece of land for maybe twenty years. It belongs to your aunts, as does everything around here. However, that makes no difference to Tutu. She's got happiness, and that's all she really wants."

We walked on. I asked Derek where he lived. He pointed beyond Tutu's house.

"In the rain forest?"

"Mildew Valley," he said cheerfully. "All that moisture and warm air. Do you know my suitcases will totally be covered with mildew in a week if I close them up in a closet?"

I wasn't sure whether he was kidding or serious. But he had already moved on to another subject. "Meganne, will I get to see you again?"

"I don't know," I replied honestly. "I'm not sure how long I'll be here."

"Going back to San Francisco?" He pulled a vine out of the way as we passed closer to the house. I reached up and started to pick one of the yellow flowers, but he firmly pushed my hand away. "Be-still tree," he said, moving his chin to indicate the yellow flowers. "Poisonous, just like oleander."

I drew my hand back. "There are sure a lot of surprises in this place. You can't tell from looking which ones are dangerous."

Later that night, lying in bed and trying to ignore the

demon's eyes in the darkened ceiling, I remembered what I'd said. Some things, it seemed, were not what they appeared. Like the pretty blue Portuguese man-of-war that had stung me so badly. I wondered if some of the people I'd met were like that: one way on the outside, quite another inside.

Suddenly, I smelled something and sat up in bed. It was raining softly outside. The trade winds were blowing through the screen door. I sniffed.

A candle, I told myself. Just been blown out. But who would have a candle in this place?

The thought of a fire in the old house made me jump out of bed, throw on a light robe, and open the door.

The hallway was damp and musty smelling. It was gloomy and dark in spite of some small wall brackets with electric lights burning weakly in them. The smell of an extinguished candle seemed everywhere. I quickly went down the hall, checking each of the doors. The rooms were empty, smelling of dust and disuse.

I was alone on the third floor of a place that seemed spookier by the minute.

I thought of going downstairs, but chided myself. My aunts had gone to sleep; I'd heard the water running in pipes and then silence. Everyone was asleep, except me and someone who had snuffed out a candle.

I pressed closer to the wall and hurried past the dim hall lights, half expecting the whole place to be plunged into darkness. I wished I'd brought a flashlight.

At the entrance to my room, I stopped. Stuck to the center of the door was a small envelope. I hadn't seen it when I'd stepped outside. Quickly I snatched it free of the candle wax that held it in place. Perhaps Aunt Marian or Tutu had slipped up and left a note, not wanting to disturb me. I closed the bedroom door behind me and walked over to the light. With fingers that trembled, I opened the envelope and stared at it in disbelief.

A single card fell into my hands. But it wasn't like any playing card I'd ever seen. A knight in armor sat on a white charger holding a staff from which flew a large flag. The flag's field was black, but there was a white flower of some sort worked into the center. Beneath the horse's hooves were lots of details, including a sailing ship, a child, what appeared to be a young woman, and a man with a miter, the headdress worn by the bishops of some churches.

A second glance showed the Roman numeral XIII and a death's head inside the armor's raised helmet.

At the bottom of the card was the single word: DEATH.

Chapter Seven

I'd never seen a tarot card, and didn't know exactly what they were, but instantly I was sure that was what I held in my hand. I remembered something about tarot cards being used in fortune telling, but I didn't believe in such things.

Yet, standing there alone in that gloomy old house isolated in the middle of the Pacific Ocean, I knew that someone had deliberately used candle wax to stick that symbol to my door as a warning.

But who?

I went quickly to the door and locked it. Even though the lock was very old, the act made me feel better. I hurried to the sliding screen and pulled the glass door across it. Then I locked it and pulled the heavy, dusty-smelling draperies. But the room was immediately stifling hot. I'd have to have some fresh air. I reached behind the heavy old draperies and opened the louvered windows at both ends of the door. It wasn't much help, but it relieved the suffocating sensation that seemed to come with the closed doors.

I tried to think calmly and rationally. What had I done

to make someone threaten me? Nothing! I had just come to ask some questions and set my own mind at rest. That couldn't be the cause of my predicament.

But who was threatening me? The only one who hadn't seemed at all friendly was Aunt Marian. Yet she couldn't have shot that arrow. Aunt Tess was even less likely. If I'd ever seen a saint, it was that fine Christian woman, confined to her wheelchair.

Tutu? The hallway was eerie and gloomy, but the floorboards had squeaked when Tutu had led me up here the first time. Her great bulk could not have passed up and down the hallway without my hearing her.

Someone else had access to this house, to the very hallway outside my door. It was a terrible feeling to know someone had been so close and I hadn't known it. In fact, if it hadn't been for smelling the candle. . . .

I debated between staying in the relative safety of my room and going downstairs to talk with Aunt Tess. She would be confined to her bed at this postmidnight hour. Tutu lifted Tess in and out of bed, but she had only been doing that since the practical nurse's death.

Somehow, I guessed, the accident that had claimed Alema's life had begun the series of events. At least, from what Tess had managed to whisper to me, it seemed that most of the trouble had started after I had phoned Tess and asked if I could come visit her and Aunt Marian for a while. Tess had sounded so glad to hear from me. She had assured me it was fine with Aunt Marian, too, although her sister wasn't at home just then. Yet Aunt Marian's aloofness when I did arrive suggested that the sisters may have had different feelings about my presence.

I paced the little room, trying to make some sense out of the problems that were enmeshing me in some kind of invisible but very real web of disaster. Somehow I sensed that my coming had upset someone's plans. It had to be that! Yet for the life of me, I couldn't think of who or why.

I shook my head at the only suspect. Aunt Marian was a strange woman, and she obviously wasn't happy about my being here, yet I couldn't imagine her doing anything really harmful. So I was right back where I started, alone, amidst strangers with unknown motives!

It couldn't be that I was an heir to the family's fortune, for many years ago my grandmother had been disinherited. Later, my mother had told me that she and I were also excluded from ever receiving any part of the Hawaiian property.

Impulsively, I decided to risk going downstairs to talk to Aunt Tess.

I kept close to the walls so the floors wouldn't squeak. I did well until I reached the bottom of the stairs and tried easing past Aunt Marian's door. Slowly I inched my way along the corridor until I was within a few feet of Tess's door.

Suddenly, Aunt Marian's door opened. I turned in fright. Aunt Marian's loose strands of hair were in greater disarray than usual. She wore a shapeless dressing gown of great age. But her dark-rimmed glasses glinted in the pale light of the spooky hallway.

"Oh, it's you, Meganne!" She sounded friendly enough. "I heard someone; you know how these old floors squeak."

"I . . . I was going to the bathroom," I stammered, instantly hating myself for lying and for being intimidated by this one old woman.

"Oh, you must be very sleepy, Meganne. It's back the other way."

I murmured my thanks and went back the way she pointed. I made a pretext of using the facilities and started back up the stairs. It wasn't until I reached the top floor that I heard Aunt Marian's door close.

I spent the rest of the night in alternating periods of

restless sleep and wide-awake fear.

But somewhere in that hot, stifling night, I came to a couple of decisions. I would not allow myself to be panicked and run back to the Mainland before I had the answers I'd come so far to get, and I would see Aunt Tess alone, somehow.

During the next week, I saw Jim Starrett off and on as he moved beyond the oleander hedge and down the trail to the beach below. He was always alone. He didn't swim much, but he walked the beach or sat under a lone palm tree for long periods. I assumed he was thinking, and yet his very aloofness concerned me. It was natural to seek other people's company. Jim didn't do that. He was a loner in actions and thoughts. I'd never known anyone like that. Still I found myself watching for him and wondered what kind of a man he really was. Since nothing more had happened to cause me fear—and I'd learned to control my thoughts at night—I decided to find out more about Jim.

One day I saw him leave his house beyond the oleanders and start down the trail. By hurrying down the vine-covered trail, I was at the bottom of the black cliff when he stepped through the brush onto the white sand beach.

"Well, hello!" he said. He wore bathing trunks and zoris, but no hat. "I've been wondering where you were, Meganne."

"Mostly staying inside out of the rain," I said. "I didn't realize it rained so much on this island."

"Doesn't, most places," he said, walking across the sand toward the lone coconut tree. "Just here in the rain forest area. But we're lucky because the wind currents or something give us more sun that just a mile or so from here, back in the Koolaus."

We sat in the shade and listened to the trade winds rattling the stiff palm fronds overhead. I found myself stealing glances at him when he was looking out to sea but still seeming to enjoy our off-and-on conversation. His wavy brown hair fell softly over his forehead, in contrast to his dominant high cheekbones and straight, Roman nose.

"How are you enjoying paradise?" he asked, bringing his eyes back to me.

I hoped that I'd glanced away before he saw me looking so closely at him. "Oh, it's kind of a mixture. I love the flowers and the blossoming trees and everything. I like the weather when it's clear but don't like the rains, especially the heavy overcast we get so much of the time. But the people are friendly."

He glanced sharply at me. "Then you haven't heard the things they say?"

"What things?"

He shrugged. "Oh, just things."

"Don't be evasive, Jim! What things? About whom?"

He studied me thoughtfully before answering. "You sure you want to know?"

"I want to know."

"Well," he said, picking up some sand and letting it drain idly through his fingers, "there's something strange going on. Maybe you've already guessed that."

I felt my heart begin to speed up.

He brushed his hands free of the sand and turned to face me squarely. "Somewhere I read that about 10 percent of the American population suffers from some kind of mental problem at one time or another in their lives. So it's probably nothing to be concerned about, but—."

"But what?" I prompted.

"You know you're living with two very strange old ladies, don't you?"

"My Aunt Tess is the finest Christian woman I've ever met."

"And your Aunt Marian?"

I hesitated. "Perhaps she's just getting a little absent-minded in her old age."

He snorted and threw up his hands. "Everyone on this island knows she hates more than anyone should. She hated her sister, your grandmother."

"How'd you know that?"

"Everyone knows. And your Aunt Marian hated your mother. She probably hates you."

"Hates me? What on earth for?"

"Because she never forgives, that's why. . . . She's probably got some loose marbles. Certainly nobody should hold a grudge for three generations."

"I can't believe you're serious, Jim Starrett!"

"Suit yourself." He snapped his mouth shut with such finality I was afraid he'd stop before telling me what I desperately wanted to know. He seemed suddenly very withdrawn, very remote and reserved.

I tried to get him started again. "Do you know how the whole thing began? I mean, with my grandmother?"

"Don't you?"

"No," I replied honestly, "I don't."

"Then it's not for me to say."

I debated what to do next. "Where can I find out?"

He shrugged again. "Ask around. Everyone knows."

"Then why won't you tell me?"

"Because I'm no *kamaaina,* no 'child of the land,' like most of the others. Some of the people around here have been listening to these tales since they were born. I've only been here a year."

I felt rebuffed and a little angry. "If you'll excuse me, I need to be getting back," I said as I stood up.

He rose slowly, seemed to hesitate, then placed both hands on my shoulders. "Meganne, I will tell you one more thing. I don't like having you around that old place."

"Why?"

He paused, then asked softly, "Can't you guess?"

I looked up at him without understanding.

Very gently and slowly he bent and kissed me. It was a surprise, and yet I found myself wanting to respond. Instead, I pushed myself away.

"I've . . . got to go," I whispered, a little unsure of myself.

"Meganne, I'd like to see you some evening soon. Like tonight. How about it?"

"That . . . would be nice, Jim."

"About eight?"

"OK."

We hesitated a moment longer. I sensed he was about to kiss me again, so I turned and walked rapidly across the white sand beach and began climbing the trail through the brush. When I cleared the top, I saw K pull the family car up to the back door. My Aunt Marian came out and got in. Then they drove away.

Suddenly, I saw my opportunity to talk to Aunt Tess alone. I waited until the car had gone through the heavy iron gate at the end of the lane, then I ran to Hale Aloha and found her sitting on the lanai.

"Meganne!" she said with a smile. "I've been praying you'd come."

"I've been wanting to see you alone for some time, Tess. I just happened to see Aunt Marian and K drive away."

"They won't be gone long. Sit down, my dear. There are some things I must tell you before it's too late."

Chapter Eight

"I'm not positive what's going on, Meganne, but I've got a pretty good idea. And it frightens me—oh, not so much for myself. I'm frightened for you."

I wondered if she knew about the arrow and the tarot card. "Tell me what happened after I called you from the Mainland," I asked quickly.

"Yes, dear. I suppose that's as good a place as any to start."

I pulled up one of the oversized chairs and sat down next to Tess's wheelchair. She looked up at me and smiled. The familiar light in her blue eyes made me feel loved.

"Well, Meganne, I guess it really started before you called, but I wasn't aware of it until after we'd talked."

Tess paused, frowning in recollection. "It seemed like an accident, so, of course, I didn't think anything about it. You see, I have an old radio in my room, above the bathtub. It's been there for years."

"That's dangerous! If it ever fell into the tub when you're taking a bath . . ."

"That's almost what happened. Alema had helped me into the tub, with the radio playing. She left the room to get something—a bar of soap, I believe—when the radio suddenly seemed to leap forward. It hit the edge of the tub and, instead of falling in with me, it fell onto the floor."

"You said the radio seemed to leap?"

"Oh, I know it sounds crazy, Meganne! But I just happened to be looking at it when it happened. It was sitting too far back on the shelf to fall of its own accord."

"Then how did it move?"

"I don't know. At the time, it didn't seem too important. Alema came running in and removed the radio. It was broken, of course. But, anyway, I just accepted that incident as something peculiar but not worth thinking about. Then after you called, and the second accident—"

She let her voice trail off. I could see she was near tears. "The accident where Alema died?"

Tess swallowed hard and spoke with difficulty. "Yes. After that, I realized the radio incident wasn't some freakish thing."

"You mean that Alema also used your bathtub, and the radio falling was really intended for her electrocution?"

"No, Meganne, my dear. Both incidents were aimed at me: the radio and the railing."

"But Alema died—?"

"Saving me. It was no accident. My wheelchair brake failed that day on the cliff top. It started to roll toward the precipice. I couldn't stop the chair. Alema was reading a few steps away, but she leaped up, grabbed for the chair, and spun it partly around. In doing so she lost her balance and fell against the railing."

"Oh, Aunt Tess! How awful!"

It took the old woman a few moments to compose herself before she could resume speaking. "By the time you arrived, I had realized what was happening. I didn't want you endangered. That's why I urged you to get away as quickly as possible."

"But why? Who would do such terrible things?"

"I don't know, Meganne. But I've prayed for wisdom according to James 1:5. I also believe that God knows the end from the beginning, and nothing can happen to me until I've finished my work here for him. At age seventy-five, that's about done."

"Nothing's going to happen to you, Aunt Tess!" I leaped up to embrace her when a windshield reflected sunlight. "It's K and Aunt Marian! They're coming back; they must-'ve forgotten something."

"More likely it's a little game, my dear. My sister probably planned it this way. I should have suspected when I saw her standing out on the cliff top, watching you with that neighbor, what's his name?"

"Jim Starrett. Aunt Marian was watching us?"

"Yes. I'm afraid she doesn't hold our neighbor in very high esteem. Anyway, my dear, you'd better hurry up to your room. My sister has been contriving to keep you and me from talking privately."

I bent quickly and gave the parchment-like cheek a quick kiss.

There were still many unanswered questions I wanted to ask Tess, but they'd have to wait. However, one other concern now nagged at me. Was that saintly old woman really in danger, too? Surely her own sister wasn't involved in anything like attempted murder! But then, nothing really made sense, including the two frightening incidents. I didn't have any idea of what motive was involved, or who—besides Aunt Marian—could possibly think of doing bodily harm to anyone.

It was with a sense of relief that I later enjoyed a quiet dinner with the two sisters without any questions or embarrassing silences. Afterwards, I excused myself and went upstairs. I wasn't sure what kind of a date Jim Starrett had in mind, so I dressed casually in a new skirt and blouse and was just starting downstairs when Aunt Marian called.

"Yes?" I said from the top of the third landing.

"You have a gentleman visitor, Meganne."

"Oh, thanks, Aunt Marian. I'll be right down."

I entered the living room with a light step, thinking about Jim's kiss and wondering how I really felt about him.

But it wasn't Jim Starrett who rose from an old chair and grinned at me.

"Hello, San Francisco! Hope you don't mind my dropping in unannounced?"

"Derek! Hi! I wasn't expecting you!"

"Well," he said, looking through his glasses with keen interest, "from the way you're dressed, I'd say you were expecting someone."

"Well, yes, as a matter of fact—."

"Say no more! I'll go quietly! After all, I should have called first."

"I'm sorry, Derek."

"It's OK, really it is. But now that I've seen how truly striking you are, how about some other time?"

"Well, yes. . . ."

"Good! There's going to be a little informal beach party with all the local people. Just a fun thing, with singing and roasting hot dogs and marshmallows, just like on the Mainland."

"I'd love it."

"Great! I'll let you know for sure which night it is."

As I walked him to the door he rubbed his sunburned nose, which tonight was only pink and not red as it had been the first time I saw him. "Could I ask who's the lucky guy, Meganne?"

I hesitated. "Well, why not? Jim Starrett."

"Jim! He's lucky at everything. Lucky at hunting, lucky

at dating, lucky at love. . . ."

"Lucky at hunting?"

"I hear he's the world's best bow hunter. Lots of wild boar in some of these islands, you know. It's considered great sport to take them with bow and arrows. . . . Uh, oh! . . . Your pretty face tells me you're one of those sensitive women who can't stand the thought of someone killing an animal. Right?"

"No, no! It's OK, Derek."

I let him out and heard him go whistling down the path. I walked back into the kitchen where my aunts looked at me with curious eyes.

"Well, Meganne," Aunt Marian said, "I must say I'm surprised to see you in here with us! What happened to your visitor?"

"He left."

"You look upset. Surely you two didn't quarrel in such a short time?"

"No, Aunt Marian. Nothing like that. I just learned something which bothers me, that's all."

"Care to talk about it? We were just going to have our evening devotions, but the Scriptures tell us to bear one another's burdens—"

"No, thanks," I said, cutting her off. My mind was pinwheeling at what Derek had said about Jim being a bowman. I felt a little shiver. Had he shot the arrow at me? If not, who had? He was certainly a logical suspect. I should have been afraid of him, yet somehow I felt a tingle of excitement. I was strangely attracted to him, and yet he was potentially threatening my life.

Suddenly, he was there. I heard him walk up to the back lanai. I was looking at Aunt Marian's mouth and saw it tighten.

"So," she said, "that's why you're dressed up and why the first gentleman caller didn't stay long."

"Yes, Aunt Marian. That's why. Jim and I are going out for a while."

I didn't invite Jim Starrett in. I didn't want to risk a scene between Jim and Aunt Marian. Anyway, I wasn't sure I could mask the doubt I now felt about him.

As soon as we were walking away from the lights of the old house, I realized I was as afraid of Jim Starrett as I was attracted to him.

I forced myself to sound lighthearted while trying to think of how to keep from being alone with him. Not that he'd harm me when three witnesses knew I was going out with him. Still, the adrenaline whipped through my body so sharply that I had to burn it up some way. Since I couldn't run, I talked.

"You've never told me about yourself, Jim."

"What's to tell? I'm a guy just trying to get along in the world."

"Doing what?"

"Writing."

"You're an author? What do you write?"

"Oh, all sorts of things."

"Such as?"

"Mysteries, mostly."

I stopped. What kind of a person wrote mysteries? Certainly someone who was interested in strange happenings, maybe even tarot cards. But I would have to be discreet to get Jim to admit any motive he might have for harming me. I looked at him. I was struggling to stay aloof and objective, but his nearness was doing strange things to my objectivity.

"What's the matter, Meganne?" Jim asked.

"Oh, nothing. I just realized you hadn't said where we're going. It would be very foolish of me not to tell my aunts. After all, I'm a guest in their house and owe them that courtesy."

Jim looked down at me with narrowed eyes that frightened me. Suddenly, I didn't want to go out with him at all.

"So," he said quietly, "now they've got you doubting me?"

I managed a laugh. "Doubting you? About what?"

"Never mind. Here! Let's just sit under the stars and talk. How about those longue chairs under the tree? See? The light from the house lets us watch each other every second. And if your aunts peer out, they can see us, sitting chastely in plain sight."

"Jim, I'm sorry if I annoyed you." Suddenly it was important he think well of me. "I'm truly sorry, Jim."

"It's OK, Meganne. I understand a whole lot more than you think I do. That's one of the advantages of being a writer."

Suddenly, two sets of eyes reflected from underneath the chaise longues. I flinched involuntarily and grabbed Jim's arm.

"Well, now," he said, putting his arm protectively around me. "When it comes to being scared of me or a couple of half-wild cats, I'm pleased you instinctively chose the cats!"

The black and white animals dashed from under the chaise longues and vanished into some ti leaves growing beside the old house.

Jim's joking manner had released the tension that had come between us. And in spite of myself, I liked the feeling of him holding me, even with one arm. "Tell me what you're writing," I said, forcing myself to move away from the warm comfort of his arm.

I saw his jaw tighten. Probably he thought I was rejecting him. I didn't know what to say, and he was silent a long moment. I kept looking at him. His face was clearly visible from the lanai light. I realized there was a rugged handsomeness about him. And when I'd clutched his arm and he had reached out to protect me, there had been something special in the touch.

Finally, Jim answered me. "I'm not superstitious—which almost everyone is on this island—but that's one thing I don't do. I mean, talk about a book I'm writing. Might jinx it."

I smiled up at him. "Thought you weren't superstitious?"

"I'm not," he said soberly, "just practical. "If I talk a story to death, I can't write it. So I think about it but don't tell it to anyone."

I was disappointed he wouldn't tell me about his writing. I wasn't quite sure I believed him, either. He just wouldn't let me inside his guard; he was still keeping that air of mystery, which fascinated and scared me in spite of my growing interest in him.

I decided to let his reasoning pass unchallenged. "What sort of beliefs do the local people have?" I asked.

"Oh, like the *menehunes*—"

"What're they?"

"Little people. Sort of like the Irish leprechauns, only not mischievious. The Hawaiians believed in the *menehunes* long before the first *haoles* landed here, and they still believe in them although not every local will admit it."

"You know a lot about Hawaii, don't you, Jim?"

"A little. But what kind of an author would I be if I didn't have a king-sized curiosity bump?"

"Have you written anything I'd be likely to know?"

"Nope. Up to now, I've written Americana and Hawaiiana and other things that only historians find interesting."

"I'd still like to know something about your books, Jim."

He looked at me in silence. In the light from the lanai, Jim's silhouette was truly handsome.

He began slowly, telling me about the missionaries and mariners who had formed Hawaii from a series of loose tribes into one people. He told me how the various birds, animals, and insects had probably come to the islands. He knew every tree, every flower.

But it was the legends that fascinated me. There were still many island people, Jim explained, who really believed in Pele, goddess of the volcanoes. In the old days, the *kahunas* or priests were known to have literally prayed people to death.

"That's impossible, Jim!"

"Not at all! The power of the human mind is beyond our understanding. The old *kahuna* simply let the victim know he was marked for death, and imagination took over."

"You mean people actually died from such things?"

"Don't act so surprised, Meganne! You know that basic human nature never changes. We get more advanced in some ways—jet planes, moon rockets, and television sets— but the rise of ancient rites like witchcraft and satanism is more pronounced today than it has been for centuries. And it all comes from the same thing."

"What's that?"

"Fear of the unknown. We're all afraid of that. Even you."

"Me?"

"Think about it, Meganne."

"But why do people get into crazy things like witchcraft and sorcery?" I asked.

"In the case of witches, it's simple: power."

"Power? I've never heard that mentioned in connection with witchcraft."

"Get some library books and read up on it, Meganne."

I hesitated. "Well, I don't know, Jim. I'd feel funny, checking such things out of a library, even if I could get to one."

"Why? Because of your faith?"

I thought about that a moment. "I've lost my faith."

"Lost it? Or temporarily laid it aside?"

I looked at him with a new sense of curiosity. He was as much as admitting that he knew about the sort of things that had been scaring me, yet he had mentioned nothing that would indicate his involvement.

"If you could look into the future," I said, ignoring his last question, "how would you do it?"

He smiled a little. "I can't see the future, Meganne. Nobody can. But that doesn't stop people from trying, and from using all kinds of ways to know and influence that future."

"Like tarot cards?"

"Tarot, Ouija boards, whatever. Some people rely on such things."

"What about you, Jim?"

He pursed his lips. "I learn to read signs. Once, I remember hearing a pastor say something that always helped me a lot. It was, 'Knowing the will of God is largely a matter of reading the signs and being willing to be led.' "

"You never mentioned a pastor before, Jim."

"No need to. Anyway, as a writer, I read signs. Not signs of the zodiac or in tea leaves or anything else, but the things around me that speak as well as words."

His voice had taken on a curiously excited edge. I looked up at him and waited for him to explain. But he didn't.

"And what signs do you read around here, Jim?"

He said very slowly and softly, "I see great danger for you, Meganne Fields. You should go home, back to the Mainland at once."

I stood nervously. "I don't have any money."

"I'll loan you some."

He said it with such fervency that I thought he really meant it. Could he really care about me? My heart raced for a moment.

"Thanks, but I can't do that."

"Think about it! Please, Meganne!" Jim spoke with such

quiet fervency that I drew back from him.

He saw the motion, stiffened, and finally stood up. "It's going to rain," he said, glancing at the sky. "I'd better take you in."

I looked up. It was true. Quietly, without my noticing it, the sky had totally clouded over. The trade winds had died down. There was a growing stillness and not a leaf moved. I glanced at the sky above the rain forest and thought I saw a faint flash of lightning.

"Yes, Jim," I said, turning toward the house. "I think it is time for me to go in."

We walked to the house together, but I felt confused. Sometimes I trusted Jim Starrett; other times I was afraid that he was part of the sinister undertone of Hale Aloha. Would I ever learn the answer to the evil that lurked within this monstrous old mansion?

Chapter 9

The next morning I took a firm grip on my nerves and forced a casual attitude as I went downstairs to breakfast with Aunt Tess and Aunt Marian.

"That was a bad storm last night, wasn't it?" I ventured. The intense lightning and violent winds had awakened me three or four times during the night.

"The telephones are out," Aunt Marian answered. "They always go out when it storms. K tells me that there was extensive damage from the storm. Would you go out and find him, Meganne? Then come back and tell me about any damage to our property."

I wasn't sure whether there was something behind her suggestion or not. I had to remind myself to stop being suspicious of everything she said or did. I told her I'd be glad to go look for K and walked out to find him.

I was surprised to see Derek in the middle of the road with K. Both were straining at a large boulder with a crowbar. "Ho!" K cried, stopping to pant from exertion. "Now we got da *kine* sistah to help us move dis boulder!"

"Hello, San Francisco!" Derek exclaimed. "Welcome to the part of Hawaii the visitor's bureau never writes about."

They showed me the damage. The stream beyond the iron gate had totally carried away the small wooden bridge. We were isolated from the rest of the island. Not that it mattered much, for there hadn't been a single outside visitor to Hale Aloha since I'd arrived.

K said the radio had announced that one man had fallen into a stream and apparently been carried out to sea. In addition a dozen cows had been swept away on the windward side as streams from the mountains had roared down normally dry canyons.

"And besides that," Derek added, "more than twenty-four inches of rain fell in that storm."

I looked at him in disbelief. He held up his right hand. "Would I lie to a pretty San Francisco girl?"

K laughed. "Depends on whether moonlight is in da *kine wahine*'s eyes."

"Speaking of moonlight," Derek said, "The party I mentioned is off—because of the storm and another reported coming. But I'll keep in touch. Meanwhile, how about going with me on a picnic this Sunday?"

"Thank you, Derek, but Sunday I go to church with my aunts."

"How about after church?"

"I don't think Aunt Marian would like it."

"Maybe if I asked her?"

"No, I don't mean that, Derek. I just mean that as a guest in her home I'd better stay close after church because there's always a Bible study and prayer time. Aunt Tess isn't quite as firm about such things, but they agree it is the Lord's day (as they put it) and everything should be in keeping with that thought."

K shook his head. "Just like the first *haole* missionaries in these islands! Very strict, you bet!"

Derek frowned. "That Aunt Marian of yours is a woman with a mind of her own, isn't she?"

I wasn't going to say anything against her, not to anyone I didn't know better than I did Derek, so I smiled. "She's always been the head of her family."

"She sure likes her power," Derek said. "A person would have to be pretty clever to outsmart that old woman. No offense intended, Meganne."

I was uncomfortable with the conversation and turned it back to safer areas. "How long will this morning's sunshine be with us?"

"Who knows? Radio says more storms are coming. It's the season."

It bothered me that we were unable to leave Hale Aloha. We were isolated by the dead phones and the rushing stream, and there was no way to leave the grounds. K saw my apprehension and assured me that a makeshift bridge would be erected, at least by Sunday morning.

"Your aunts have never missed a church service because the bridge's been out yet," he told me.

But my thoughts continued to wander. Was whoever was threatening our lives also imprisoned on the top of this cliff? I still wondered if Aunt Marian was behind everything, but if so, she obviously had help.

"Hey, sistah!"

K's voice jarred me into awareness. "I'm sorry, K. What were you saying?"

"I said, 'You'd better move because Derek and I have worked this boulder loose and you're right in the way of where it'll roll.'"

I hastily backed up and they used the crowbar to force the boulder off the road. I glanced up at the boulders that still clung to their position overhead. It'd be easy for one of them to smash down on someone, I thought. Then I immediately checked myself for thinking such a thing.

"Where do you live, Derek?" I asked when he'd stopped to catch his breath.

He leaned against the crowbar and waved toward a jungle of huge trees and trailing vines the opposite direction from Jim Starrett's place. "A small shack with a leaky tin roof back over there."

"On Hale Aloha property?"

"Oh, no! Way beyond that."

"Don't you work for my Aunt Marian?"

"Who, me?" Derek laughed. "I don't work for anybody."

"Then why're you helping K with this debris?"

"Why am I helping you, K?"

The big islander grinned. "Ho! I tell you why, bruddah! You afraid I tell dis *kine wahine* about you, tell her true!"

The words were spoken in obvious jest, but I saw a flicker of concern cross Derek's eyes. Or had I imagined that? I gathered that K was a rather easy-going type of man who didn't get upset about anything. But I couldn't decide what I thought of Derek. I waited until they were removing some debris from across the driveway to ask what kind of work he did.

"Me?" Derek threw a handful of vines beside the driveway. "Didn't you hear Tutu? I'm a beach bum!"

"No, seriously," I said.

Again Derek's eyes seemed to tell me more than his words. But instead of answering my question he smiled and stooped to pick up more brush to throw away.

K answered for him. "He works off and on in the hospital on the windward side. He knows a little about pharmacy but he also knows a little about everything."

Derek grinned and discarded the compliment with an airy wave of his tanned arms. "Jack-of-all-trades and master of none, you know."

K grunted. "Ho! Don't you believe him, Meganne! Nothing Derek can't do. Hey, tell her about the crazy people work with you Derek!"

I could see Derek wasn't into talking about himself. Still, he managed a smile and started telling about some of the women who worked in the little hospital. "One's into occult. Another fought with this one about having a 'black aura,' as she called it. So one day I mentioned this to the supervisor and she said, 'They're nuts, those two. Me, I'm into voodoo!' "

I looked at him as K laughed at the story he'd obviously heard before. "You're kidding me, aren't you, Derek?"

He shook his head solemnly. "Everybody's nuts these days. Why, there's even one guy I know who's into poltergeists."

"You mean he believes in playful spirits who throw things?"

Derek looked somberly at me. "My friend says poltergeists are not always so friendly."

I remembered that remark Sunday.

Another light storm had kept the bridge from being repaired enough for the car to pass over, so we'd walked across on a makeshift foot bridge. The phones had begun working again, so someone had been contacted to drive up to the other side of the bridge to get us. I was feeling pretty good, for nothing more had happened to scare me. I had half-convinced myself there was nothing to fear, but I was still determined to leave Hale Aloha as soon as I had the necessary money and the answers I had come for.

We drove down out of the rain forest to Oahu's windward side to attend church. The pastor was Korean. He'd been converted in his homeland, studied on the Mainland, and been assigned to this small congregation in the middle of the Pacific Ocean.

As we seated ourselves Tess whispered that Pastor Kim was solidly evangelical. That meant she approved, because his theology was Bible-based and Christ-centered. I personally was a little uneasy with that concept, since I'd "fallen from grace," as Aunt Marian had once expressed it.

After the singing and other preliminaries, Pastor Kim arose, affixed his lavaliere microphone to his black robe, and looked seriously at his audience. There weren't many white people. Most were race variations—brown and yellow islanders who blended together into a common unit of Christians.

"I wish to speak to you this morning on a subject that should have been left in ancient history," the minister began. "But this subject did not die then, or even with the Salem witch hunts of early American history. It is because those forces are not dead that I must speak frankly this morning."

His text was the same one I'd seen marked in my room. "For we wrestle not against flesh and blood. . . ."

I glanced at Aunt Tess. She wore an out-of-style straw hat that partially shielded her face, and she was nodding in agreement. So was Aunt Marian, which surprised me a little. I couldn't make up my mind what I really thought about her faith—or lack of it.

It was obvious that Aunt Marian was in accord with the pastor's comments that Satan was alive and lived in the hearts of modern men and women.

"Dr. Billy Graham has said that there is currently the greatest in-gathering of souls in centuries," Pastor Kim said. "But at the same time, we have seen a corresponding rise in satanic forces. In this modern age, the newspapers carry daily horoscopes. We read and hear of terrible murders and other terrors, which have come to the attention of the authorities because of some motive involving black magic, satanism, the occult, and voodoo."

Ordinarily, I'd not have cared for such a sermon topic. But this was a modern preacher who was dealing with a subject as old as mankind, and yet as new as the morning newspaper or radio newscast.

"In last month's newspaper," Pastor Kim went on, "there was a feature story about a local coven of witches. Some of you saw the picture, I'm sure. The head witch was a beautiful young woman. Those pictured with her were ordinary-looking people. There were no wild-eyed types among them. And that's what is so frightening."

He went on to say that at the last ministerial association meeting there had been considerable discussion about the resurgence of the old Hawaiian religions with their *kahunas*. "The association was divided on whether to speak about this subject from the pulpit or not," Pastor Kim said, looking over the top of his dark-rimmed glasses at his small congregation. "We weren't sure whether it was better to ignore the rising tide of evil in our midst, as many pastors are doing for fear of giving even more attention to the subject, or whether it was better to alert the people so they might put on the whole armor of God, as Paul advises. With great reluctance, and after prayerful consideration, I have decided upon the latter course."

Tutu was leaning forward, her great bulk cooled by a bulletin waved as a fan in her plump hands. K wasn't there. Neither was Malia or Derek. But away back in the corner by the door, as though he had slipped in late, Jim Starrett was frowning in dark, gloomy concentration. I was frankly surprised to see him in church.

What the pastor went on to recite scared me. A few weeks ago I would have dismissed the whole thing as irresponsible and weird, but I could not forget what was being said this morning.

Pastor Kim declared that people usually got into the occult, witchcraft, satanism, and the like through seemingly innocent things. He cited Ouija boards as an example, and warned about Christians reading the daily horoscopes in the newspaper.

"It becomes a runaway train going down a steeper and steeper grade," the pastor said. "A train from which you cannot jump. You are headed for doom unless you call upon the Lord Jesus Christ."

I listened with a strange fascination as the pastor continued on. "The Bible teaches obedience and taking up the cross. It teaches submission to authority. It teaches putting others first. And that is all contrary to what prompts people into the black arts. These people want power. They want authority. They want to control others—to bend them to their will—and that often means by fear and intimidation. But naturally, there comes a time when some people will not yield to fear and threats."

The pastor cited some cases I hadn't heard about. There had been a few ritualistic murders that the authorities had traced to suspects involved in the occult. There had also been other murders, which some authorities believed were tied into satanism. The victims had not yielded to the threats, and, unable to abandon the runaway train on which they'd embarked, were forced into the murdering of innocent people.

I felt goosebumps run up and down my spine. What he was saying seemed all too close to my own life. The strange goings-on at Hale Aloha hinted of both witchcraft and murder.

"You've all read in the papers this past year about what the reporters call the 'Flying Devil.' Witnesses at one of his terrible crimes say he spread great wings, which stretched from his shoulders and upraised arms to his knees. Authorities believe the killer wore a military rain poncho, but some of the witnesses are still convinced he was a fiend with wings. Whoever or whatever he is, he's killed three young women in what police call 'occult' cases, and he's still at large."

The congregation stirred restlessly.

"But the tragic thing is that many believing Christians are innocently going along today, not believing there is any such thing as demons, although our Lord cast them out and the Scripture clearly teaches the existence of such creatures," the pastor concluded. "And other Christians, quite innocently, get involved in the occult by failing to see the harm in it. Theirs is a supermarket religion, where they pick out of God's Word what they want, and choose to disbelieve or ignore other clear teachings of our Savior."

Pastor Kim invited those who wanted to "put on the whole armor of God" to "quench the fiery darts of the wicked" to come forward for prayer.

For the first time in a long time, I felt my heart stirred. I thought about the public confession of faith I had made some years ago, about losing my faith as a result of the broken romances, and I thought about reaffirming my belief in Jesus Christ. But I sat quietly and the service ended without me being among those who walked down to the front of the little church.

I turned to look over my shoulder at Jim Starrett. I wondered what he believed. But he was gone. He had slipped out. It was as though he'd never been there. However, I knew he had, and I wondered why he had left so quickly after the benediction.

I pushed Tess's wheelchair into the narthex after the line of worshipers had shaken hands with the pastor and gone outside to the open lanai for coffee. Tess introduced me to Pastor Kim while Aunt Marian lingered behind to speak to several women.

"Pastor Kim," I said, shaking his hand, "I must confess I never expected to hear a sermon like yours today."

He smiled. "One of Satan's favorite tricks is to make us believe he does not exist, Miss Fields. He convinces us we are too well educated, too intelligent to believe such things. But you can see that the heart of mankind never

changes. Just read the papers and look around you. Then be
sure you've taken the protection God has provided us
through his Word."

I moved on, pushing Tess's wheelchair and acknowledg-
ing the various introductions she made of our fellow worshipers. But my mind was still in the sanctuary, beginning
to wonder about things that my logical brain had never
doubted before I had arrived at Hale Aloha. Even though
the sun was shining and the day was very warm, I felt a chill
I couldn't explain.

Chapter Ten

While I'd been talking to Pastor Kim, Aunt Marian had been making arrangements for a new practical nurse to take care of Aunt Tess. Ingrid was not a member of the local church, but several parishioners had recommended her, and she'd been visiting the church that day. Aunt Marian quickly interviewed Ingrid, checked with Tess, and hired her as a replacement for the late Alema.

That turned out to be a break for me, for Ingrid was a true Hawaiian *kamaaina*, or 'child of the land.' We had a brief moment alone after she arrived with her bags.

"I am a Christian woman," she said, looking down on me from her six feet of bone and muscle, "and a good nurse to nice old ladies like your Aunt Tess. I have never been in this old house although I have heard so much about it."

"You have, Ingrid?"

"Of course! My grandfather came here from Germany to oversee the cane and pineapple plantations. I was born near Pearl Harbor. Because I am a good listener, I have learned many things in the homes where I have worked. I went to school here. I know every legend, every story, everything—good and bad."

"Then you know more about this old mansion than I, Ingrid. It seems to have some secret that I can't learn."

"I know the mystery of Aloha House, Meganne."

"Sometime I'd like you to tell me—everything."

"You are not afraid, *liebchen?*"

"Should I be?"

"Not if you are a Christian."

I didn't say anything. In the momentary lull, I heard my aunts coming. Marian was pushing Tess's chair through the far room.

"I'm not afraid, Ingrid."

"Then I will tell you sometime soon." She raised her voice. "I will push the chair! I am all ready to work."

A few days later, I had an opportunity to speak with Ingrid further when Ingrid drove us into Honolulu to take Aunt Tess for a routine checkup. Aunt Marian had gone down the street to do some shopping while her sister was in the doctor's office, which left Ingrid and me alone. We went outside and walked around the medical center grounds.

Everything was beautiful under a typical Hawaiian sky of intense blue with magnificent white cumulous clouds rising over the Koolaus. The center grounds were ablaze with flowering trees and shrubs. Red, pink, and purple bougainvillea climbed over old coral fences. It was too pretty a day to talk about dark things; but I wanted to learn the truth, so I immediately asked Ingrid to tell me about Hale Aloha.

"Your Aunt Marian thinks I am too blunt-speaking," Ingrid began, "but I am not afraid of her. And I don't think many people can say that, can they, *liebchen?*"

"I'm not afraid of her, either."

Ingrid smiled down at me. "Aren't you, Meganne?"

I examined my inner thoughts and decided not to commit myself. Instead, I said, "Tell me about everything, Ingrid."

"Where does gossip begin and facts stop?" Ingrid wondered. "I'm a Christian woman who struggles with such questions."

"My father was a newspaper editor, and he always just told things as he learned them, citing his source. Would that be fair for you?"

"That sounds fair," Ingrid agreed. "But I will stop when I am unsure if it would be wrong to say something. All right?"

I agreed.

"Captain Joel Hendrix was a sea captain who feared nothing, absolutely nothing. He had made his money black-birding and so was acquainted with the superstitions of the black people he hauled across the seas in his ships. He wasn't above kidnaping some Hawaiians when he sailed this way. From them, he learned about their beliefs. But they meant nothing to him, and to show his own powers were greater than anything he couldn't see, he settled here, deliberately building Hale Aloha on the site of an old Hawaiian *heiau,* or pagan temple, where human sacrifices had been offered.

"Captain Hendrix married a woman named Hester, the daughter of a former missionary whose wife had died and who had turned to being a ship's chandler. Hendrix sailed to San Francisco, bought a Queen Anne Victorian mansion, and had it dismantled. It was marked so that it could be completely reassembled in Hawaii. He named the house Hale Aloha—house of love—for Hester.

"She later bore him three daughters, which was a sore spot to Hendrix, who thought his manliness should have produced sons. One of the girls was your grandmother, Meganne." Ingrid touched my hand, almost as if she felt sorry for me.

"The Hawaiians were offended by Hendrix's outrage to their pagan—but to them, sacred—grounds. They said their *kahunas* were going to pray Mrs. Hendrix to death. When she died a short time later, they said it was because the priests' powers were greater than the *haole* sea captain's.

"Hendrix became bitter in his advancing years and ran off all his daughters' suitors. Marian became much like her father, stern and domineering. She easily controlled Tess, but the youngest daughter, Margaret, was openly hostile to both her aging father's will and her oldest sister's wishes. Soon Margaret brought a young man home with her. The family was polite, but that's about all. And then something happened."

Ingrid paused in her narrative and I asked, "What?"

She looked soberly across the Pacific, which stretched out in blue green beauty toward some low white clouds on the horizon. "Marian fell in love with Margaret's boyfriend."

"She what?"

"Your Aunt Marian fell for her younger sister's fiance. There was a terrible scene, and finally the boyfriend took Margaret to the Mainland. There they were married. Your mother was born, and of course, eventually, so were you."

I searched Ingrid's face. She was telling the truth, I knew. "So that's why Aunt Marian disliked my mother and grandmother so much! But how can she hate me after all these years? I wasn't responsible. I didn't even know about it!"

Ingrid shrugged. "Your Aunt Marian believes she's a good Christian. I've heard her say that very thing. But she doesn't know her Bible, unless she ignores the part about 'He who says he loves God and hates his brother is a liar.'"

It was about time to be getting back to the doctor's office, but I was too enthralled to let Ingrid stop just yet.

"Ingrid," I said softly, "I've got to know something."

"Yes, what do you need to know, *liebchen?*"

"Have you ever heard some—some rumors about my mother?"

"You mean that she was possessed?"

I nodded, then added, "I don't believe in demon possession. Do you?"

"I do not know, Meganne. Sometimes my mind tells me that it is not so. But my Bible tells me differently. Can I believe part of the Bible and not all? If so, which part shall I believe and which shall I not?"

"But demon possession in this century? It's crazy!"

"I do not know, *liebchen.* Some movies have been made about demon possession, and the antichrist as a child, and people have flocked to see them. I can't help but think people today believe in demons, devils, and evil spirits just as much—deep down inside—as the locals here believe in Pele, goddess of the volcano, and *menehunes* and other ancient beliefs."

"But my mother—?"

"Those were always whispered words, Meganne. No one could say who started such rumors, or who kept them going."

I felt anger begin to rise inside me. But I had known the frustration so often I could answer with control. "Ingrid, I believe those rumors helped kill my mother. And I know they twice wrecked my chances for a happy marriage."

I told her briefly about my experiences, concluding, "I finally decided there was nothing to do but come here and find out the truth."

"And what," Ingrid asked me softly, "is the truth, *liebchen?*"

I thought about that as we walked back across the grounds to the doctor's office. "Tell me one more thing before we go inside, Ingrid. What do you know about the other people around my great-aunts? Malia, Jim, K, and yes, Derek, just for example."

"Your Great-Aunt Marian thinks Malia can do no harm, although almost everyone else knows she's into witchcraft."

I stopped and stared unbelievingly at Ingrid. "Malia?"

"Didn't you know, *liebchen*?"

"No, Ingrid. I didn't know. In fact, I'm sorry to say I still can't believe that."

"The people who practice witchcraft today are not old crones with black hats and broomsticks. You remember what Pastor Kim said about the picture of a modern coven in the newspaper? Well, I know two of those women, and they are seemingly ordinary people. Until I saw them in the paper, I didn't know they were into witchcraft."

I wanted to pursue the subject further, but we were at the door, and I could see a nurse pushing Tess's wheelchair down the hallway toward the waiting room. "What about the young men around Hale Aloha?"

Ingrid pursed her lips thoughtfully. "K is what they call locally a 'Buddahead.' He uses the term himself sometimes. He's a Buddhist of Japanese-Hawaiian descent who doesn't have a mean bone in his body. He's superstitious, of course, as many locals are. But he's a nice man."

"And Derek?"

Ingrid frowned. "He's a strange one. Works in the hospital doing menial tasks when he's not on the beach fishing."

"You mean surfing?" I corrected.

"No, fishing. He's a brilliant kid, but there's something strange about him. I can't explain it," Ingrid said, "but he's that way. I hear he's determined to finish something once he starts it. That's why some people think he'll get what he's after right now."

I let a few people pass me and enter the waiting room before I asked, "What is he after, Ingrid?"

"Malia."

"Malia? I don't understand what you mean."

"He's making a determined effort to get her to marry him."

I stopped and Ingrid did the same. I asked, "Derek is trying to marry Malia?"

"Does that surprise you, *liebchen?*"

"Yes, as a matter of fact, it does." I started to tell her about the interest Derek had seemed to show in me, but decided to skip that. Maybe I'd been fooling myself. Or maybe Derek was just having some fun at my expense.

"What about Jim Starrett, Ingrid?"

She frowned. "He says he's a writer, but nobody really knows his background."

I saw Tess looking at us through the glass door. But questions were still burning inside me.

"Why do you think those rumors about my mother never cropped up until I was getting serious about a boy?"

She shrugged. "I don't know, *liebchen.* But I could make a guess if it weren't liable to be construed as gossip."

"Aunt Marian!"

Ingrid shrugged. "I'm not saying anything more, Meganne. But if I were you, I'd do what Pastor Kim suggested and 'put on the whole armor of God.' " Ingrid opened the door and we entered the waiting room.

Tess was wheeling her chair toward us. "You two must have been having a very interesting discussion."

"Just talking," I said. "What did the doctor say?"

The old face sobered. "I can't believe it. He says I have high blood pressure and must start taking some special medication. He gave me a prescription." Tess held up a small slip of paper that looked harmless.

But indirectly that piece of paper brought death into our lives.

Chapter Eleven

We picked up Aunt Marian, filled Aunt Tess's prescription (a medication Ingrid said she had administered to patients before), and returned to Hale Aloha. But my attitude had changed, for I'd learned something about my aunts and this strange old mansion isolated by time, distance, and both natural and man-made barriers.

In my own mind, I knew Aunt Marian had managed to wreck my romances. But that meant she had to have some tie to the Mainland, and especially to the area where my mother and I had lived.

Why had she done such a thing? Slowly a plausible, yet implausible, answer came to me. She must be unbalanced.

Either that, or she's . . . possessed!

As that word came to me, I recoiled in disgust. Meganne Fields, that's the word that ruined your mother's life—and yours! Stop it!

I really didn't believe there was anything to demon possession . . . or did I? I found myself turning more and more to the Bible to check references that I had always dismissed as nonsense. Was it possible I was dealing with the occult at Hale Aloha?

Or was it possible that hate had unhinged Aunt Marian's mind?

Much as I preferred to believe the latter, I began to study the Bible with the help of Aunt Tess's concordance.

I looked under witches because Malia was rumored to be one. The Old Testament showed strong disapproval, saying, "Thou shalt not suffer a witch to live." If the Bible was trustworthy, then there had to be witches . . . if not today, then in earlier times.

Samuel had been dead a long time when Saul lost his faith and sought out a woman who had a "familiar spirit." My King James Version didn't call her a witch, but the headline said: "Saul, forsaken of God, seeketh a witch." This woman at Endor had "brought up" Samuel from the dead, and his consultation with spirits was one of the things that led to Saul's death.

I realized I was scaring myself by reading only these verses referring to witches. But somehow driven to continue, I turned to the New Testament.

Witches weren't mentioned under that name, but Paul dealt with a man who was using a young woman with some sort of psychic powers. I also looked up demons. Jesus not only cast them out, but he gave the disciples power over them. "And these signs shall follow them that believe," Jesus had said in Mark 16:17, "In my name shall they cast out devils."

How could Jesus say something that wasn't true? While I still felt that God had let me down by permitting the loss of both my parents at so young an age, and allowing my romances to be broken, I still knew that he existed and that the Scriptures were his way of communicating with human beings.

I sat up with a start. Was I still a believer in spite of

thinking I had lost my faith?

I had been reading under a palm tree near the beach. When I looked up from my books I saw Derek fishing in the surf. I got to my feet and walked over to the water, calling to him.

"Well, hello, San Francisco," he answered, shifting his pole so he could wave at me. His nose was covered with a white ointment, but the sunburn was still obvious. "Where'd you come from?"

I motioned back toward the low palm. "Over there. I was reading."

"Anybody ever warn you about getting knocked on the head by one of those falling coconuts?"

I laughed. "No. Should I be concerned?"

"Not unless one falls. Then nobody will have to warn you."

"I'll keep that in mind." I looked closely at the tips of his fishing pole. "How do you catch fish without a line?"

"There's a line," he said. "Walk up and feel it."

He lowered the pole and I felt the line. "It's amazing. It's invisible until I'm inches from it."

"Special line I perfected myself," Derek said with pride. "Fools the fish even better than you."

"I see what you mean," I said as Derek suddenly jerked his pole, waited expectantly, and then shook his head.

"A strike, but I missed him."

I wanted to know about his relationship with Malia, so I said, "Seen Malia lately?"

He nodded, watching the end of his pole as though he expected the fish to try again. "Here and there," he replied.

That wasn't very helpful. "You seem well liked by her parents."

"I like everyone; everyone likes me, so why not?"

"I'd like to know all of them better."

Derek grinned. "Sure, you would!"

I was annoyed for some reason. "Why do you say that?"

"Because, San Francisco, her father's ideas and Malia's may not agree with yours. For example, did you know her father believes he's a *kahuna,* a priest of the old Hawaiian line?"

"You mean a witch doctor?"

"*Haole* term! *Kahuna* is a very ancient Hawaiian word."

"And . . . Malia?"

"Ask her yourself." He jerked his head toward the cliff.

I turned to look as a voice called above the surf's sound. I saw Malia moving across the white sand. She wore a fitted muumuu, which showed off her trim figure to advantage. I glanced at Derek, remembering what Ingrid had said about his intentions toward Malia. But he didn't show any special signs of emotion.

"There you are, Meganne!" Malia said as she walked closer. "Your Aunt Tess was looking for you."

She smiled and tried to make her voice sound friendly, but I had the distinct impression she wasn't too happy to see me talking with Derek.

"I'd better go in and see what she wants," I said. "Thanks for bringing the message." I smiled at Derek, trying not to seem overly friendly or unfriendly. "See you."

"Sure," he replied.

I walked across the beach to the volcanic cliff and started up the trail. When I glanced back, I sensed something in Malia's and Derek's stances that suggested they were quarreling.

I approached Tess where she was sitting on the lanai behind the guard rail at the top of the cliff. She was gazing across the ocean lost in thought. Ingrid was dozing nearby.

"Hi! You wanted to see me?"

The old woman smiled. "I always want to see you, Meganne. Sit down." She patted a chaise longue.

"You didn't send for me?"

Tess frowned slightly. "No. I don't think so. But sometimes I don't remember too well. Sit down anyway and let's talk."

I eased into the longue and looked out to sea. It was a beautiful sight. The heavy white clouds were ringed on the horizon. Between there and us was an incredibly blue green ocean. A speck of foam indicated that a small vessel was moving across the surface.

"It's so pretty here, Tess," I said after a long silence.

"It truly is," she agreed. "I sometimes come here to pray and think."

"Were you praying just now?"

"Yes, Meganne. The doctor's examination yesterday made me think of something I've never really allowed myself to think about before."

"What's that?"

Tess glanced at the big bulk of Ingrid. She was obviously asleep, her head tilted back slightly and her open mouth emitting deep snores.

"I'm thinking of defying my sister."

I sat up and leaned forward. "Did the doctor tell you something you're not telling us?"

"Nothing too unusual, really. He just made me aware that my time is short."

"Tess!" I jumped up and put my arms around her skinny old shoulders.

She touched my hands lovingly. "Nothing to worry about, my dear. Nothing unusual; I'm just getting along in years, and the need for the new medication reminded me that I'm ready, spiritually, to meet my Savior. It also made me think of something else. . . . Meganne, I'm going to do something against your Aunt Marian's wishes."

I released my arms and knelt beside Tess's wheelchair. "You're serious, aren't you, Tess."

"Very serious."

"And you've never defied her before, have you?"

"Never."

I hesitated a moment, wondering if I should ask something that really wasn't my business. But Tess had obviously brought up the subject because she wanted to talk about it. "What are you going to do, Tess?"

She didn't answer at first. Instead, she turned her wheelchair slightly so her view would take in the house. Aunt Marian was walking out the back door with a pitcher of milk. She poured some into a couple of small tin plates. The two semiwild cats were nowhere in sight.

"Aunt Marian can't hear you from here, if that's what you're wondering," I assured Tess.

"I know," she replied, but still hesitated.

I didn't want to push her, so I kept silent, wondering what could possibly make this saintly old woman risk the wrath of her older sister. "We don't have to talk about it, Tess," I finally said gently.

"It's about you, Meganne, so of course you should know. But I'm just not sure you would be safe if you knew."

Tess looked at me a long time, searching my eyes. She was concerned for me; I sensed that with some alarm. Suddenly, I didn't really want to know what was in that wonderful woman's heart.

"Perhaps you'd better pray some more about it," I suggested.

"Perhaps so," she agreed. "I'll wait until morning."

We let the subject drop, but it hung heavily between us as we sat there together, gazing at the Pacific below us. I began to have some quick, prickly thoughts about Tess's own welfare if she defied her sister. If I was right, and Aunt Marian wasn't emotionally stable, my favorite relative could be in jeopardy.

My eyes caught movement up by the house. The two semiwild cats slid silently out of the underbrush and advanced cautiously toward the container of milk Aunt Marian had put out for them.

"Do those cats have names?" I asked.

Tess smiled faintly. "Black and white; good and evil."

I glanced sharply at Tess. "Are those really their names?"

"No, Meganne, of course not! We never named them. I was just thinking out loud, that's all."

I spent the rest of the afternoon wondering about the conversation with Tess, and trying to forget the representation of those two cats as good and evil.

Later, I sat on the edge of my bed, thinking about all I'd learned that day. I realized, somehow, that whatever Tess was contemplating involved me, and, she said, it placed me in danger.

Suddenly as I looked at the dresser a bottle of perfume I'd had sitting on the nightstand crashed to the floor, filling the room with fragrance. I cleaned up the mess, remembering what Tess had said about her radio.

Later, as I was about to turn off the light, a bottle of cologne suddenly shattered beside me.

What in the world! I wondered. Both of the objects hadn't fallen straight down as they would have if I'd left them too close to the edge. They had sailed well away from their resting places as though they'd been thrown—just as Aunt Tess's radio had "fallen off" the shelf.

I didn't sleep much that night. I tried not to think of the word that kept coming to mind, and which my logical brain kept rejecting: poltergeist.

The next morning I could hardly wait to share my rising fears and doubts with Tess. But when Ingrid left her alone on the lanai for a moment, I couldn't speak before the saintly old woman smiled at me.

"Meganne," she said softly, "I've been praying much of the night. I've decided to do it."

"Do what?" I asked, my mind on my own concerns.

Tess glanced around to make sure we were alone, and then whispered, "I've decided to change my will."

"You've what?"

"Shh! I'm going to name you as my beneficiary, Meg-anne!"

Chapter Twelve

So that was why Aunt Marian had been so cool to me when I had arrived. That's why she had tried to keep me from seeing Aunt Tess alone.

"I first mentioned the thought," Tess continued, "after you called from the Mainland. But I backed down," she admitted. "The day you arrived I discussed it with Marian again."

I remembered the faint sounds of quarreling I had heard my first night at Aloha House.

"But who is the present heir," I asked Tess, almost afraid to hear her answer.

Tess looked at me and spoke so softly that I was not sure whether I read the word on her lips or heard her say it.

"Malia."

For a while only the distant surging of the ocean broke the ominous silence that hung between us.

Then Tess continued. "As the will now stands, the surviving sister inherits everything. However, we had agreed that no matter which of us was the last survivor—Marian or me—the inheritance would go to Malia."

The old woman paused, her eyes moist. "But I've never been comfortable with that. There are two Scriptures that seem to speak to me, although they aren't specifically written to aunts, of course."

Tess quoted them. " 'A good man leaveth an inheritance to his children's children,' from Proverbs 13:22. And then from I Timothy 5:8, 'But if any provide not for his own, and especially those of his own house, he hath denied the faith, and is worse than an infidel.' "

The old woman paused, her eyes wet. "You are the only person besides Marian who is 'of my own house,' Meganne."

I reached out and hugged her. We clung silently together for a moment.

"Aunt Tess, you don't have to do that for me."

"I know I don't have to, legally. But I'm convinced it's right in God's eyes. My sister doesn't agree, but I'm going to do it anyway, just as soon as I can."

"But—," I said, and then stopped. A frightening thought struck me. If Aunt Marian had hated three generations for forty years, she would not allow anything to change now.

I was quite sure that Aunt Tess's decision solidly threatened me and possibly even herself. If anything happened to her now, before the will was changed, Marian's wishes would prevail. I closed my eyes, trying to blot out a horrible picture of both Aunt Tess and me dead, probably by some "accident."

But what could I do? If I ran, Aunt Tess would be vulnerable, except for Ingrid. Certainly I was in a precarious position, because I was alone except for what little help I might have from those around Hale Aloha. I needed to trust someone besides Aunt Tess. But who? Ingrid? Possibly, but conceivably her life could also be endangered. No, I needed someone outside the house.

There were only three possibilities: K, Derek, and Jim. I didn't know K that well. Besides, he was Aunt Marian's employee. That left only two. I was afraid of Jim. He was supposed to be a bowman, and I hadn't forgotten the arrow fired so close to me. But dared I trust Derek, whom I knew to be involved with Malia?

Aunt Tess broke my thoughts. "Meganne, there's one thing more I must say to you."

I forced my thoughts to stay away from the situation that threatened our lives. "What's that, Aunt Tess?"

"I gather you've lost your faith in our Savior?"

With a sigh, I nodded. I didn't want to go into my reasons, not now, with more pressing matters swirling madly about me.

"But you have previously made a public confession of faith, Meganne?"

"Yes. Once. And I've always gone to church."

"Church isn't the same thing, you know. Jesus said, 'Ye must be born again.' Were you ever, really, Meganne?"

Tess saw the doubt in my eyes. "It's really quite simple, Meganne. Mark tells us that Jesus first began his ministry by saying, 'Repent and believe the Gospel.' Later, Jesus told Nicodemus, 'You must be born again.' "

"I know all those things, Aunt Tess," I interrupted as gently as possible.

"You know them intellectually, my dear. But they must become part of your heart. Paul said, 'If you confess with your mouth Jesus as Lord, and believe in your heart that God raised him from the dead, you shall be saved."

"I've also heard that, Aunt Tess. Many times, in fact: repent, believe, receive, be baptized."

"Do you want to do that, Meganne?"

I shrugged and looked away. "Not now, I guess. But I do know one thing for sure." I turned back to face the old woman with deep concern.

"What's that, my dear?"

"My number one need right now—and yours—is the protection of our lives. I'm afraid of Aunt Marian!"

Tess slowly shook her head. "I don't believe that, my dear. My sister is eccentric, perhaps, but she'd not harm anyone physically. She just doesn't control her tongue as well as I'd like. But harm you or me? Nonsense!"

For a moment, I considered that. Aunt Marian certainly hadn't fired that arrow at me. She wasn't strong enough. But she could have left the tarot card. On the other hand, how would she have known about such things? Still, I had no doubt she was involved—but with an accomplice. I shivered.

"Are you cold, Meganne?"

"Huh? No, I was just thinking. Please excuse me, Aunt Tess, I have some things I need to do."

I wanted to be alone, but not in the confines of my room in Hale Aloha. So I put on my tennis shoes and walked down the path to the beach toward the lone palm tree by the surf.

I had barely seated myself in the shade when Jim Starrett came wading in from the sea. "Aloha, Meganne," he said, pausing just outside the palm tree's shade. "Am I interrupting?"

"No, not really."

He hesitated. I hadn't invited him to sit down. "Sorry to disturb you, Meganne," he said, and started across the sand toward the black cliff.

"You didn't disturb me." Was that me saying that? I wanted to be alone, to think. I especially didn't want to be around this man right now. And yet I was strangely fascinated by him.

He didn't want to talk about himself. When I asked, he shrugged and said, "Not much to tell." I tried again, asking how he'd become interested in writing. Had he been a newspaperman like my father?

Jim shook his head and ran bronzed fingers through his wet hair. "No. I did a lot of other things, though."

"Such as?"

"Oh, the usual, I guess. Lumberjack. Driving a truck. Working odd jobs here and there."

That was curious. An extremely masculine man with a creative mind? My father had always said that the reporters and writers he knew were readers and not doers.

"You like to hunt, Jim?"

"I've done some. Fished a little, too."

"You must be good to hunt with a bow and arrow." It was a wild shot, but I had an opportunity to slip it in, and was anxious for Jim's reaction.

He smiled a little and shook his head shortly. "I'm not that good, Meganne."

"But you are an archer, aren't you?"

His suspicions were aroused. He looked steadily at me, and I felt a sense of cold fear begin deep inside me. "Now what on earth made you ask that, Meganne Fields?"

I tried to laugh it off, to indicate it was an idle question, but his brooding, somber eyes told me he didn't believe me. He was cautious after that, and the conversation deteriorated into longer and longer lapses between meaningless words.

He rose, brushed the sand from his still-damp legs and said, "Well, sorry I disturbed you, Meganne Fields. See you later."

He walked off without a backward glance. I shivered a little in the warm air, but I wasn't sure why. I felt a little like a bird hypnotized by a snake; I also felt I was being unjust in thinking about Jim Starrett as anything other than a handsome young man. After all, I didn't have one shred of proof he wasn't a fine person. I guessed it was his moody ways, his secretiveness, that made me afraid. And yet the attraction toward him grew in spite of myself.

I tried to force myself to think of the pressing issue before me. I was in danger. I knew that. I should think about getting away. But the more I tried, the more I found myself thinking about Jim Starrett and wondering what secret he was hiding.

"Hey, San Francisco!" Derek Norton came bounding across the sand from the brush at the end of the black cliff. He was carrying his fishing pole.

I waved and he stopped in the shade. The palm fronds rattled overhead as the trade winds passed through them.

"That beach party I told you about is on again for tonight. Want to come?"

I looked up and squinted against the brightness of the sky beyond his head. "I don't think so, Derek. Thanks anyway."

He squatted before me. "Something bothering you, San Francisco?"

"Oh, no, not really. I just don't feel in the mood for a party, I guess."

"Too bad. Well, invitation's open. Very informal group. If you change your mind, just wander down. It's hard to resist Hawaiian music on a moonlight night. And we should have a good one."

"If it doesn't rain."

"No rain in sight, radio says. But there's a big storm building up far out over the Pacific. Better have a good time while you can."

He rose, smiled, and went on down the beach to the surf. I felt a little rebuffed. He hadn't shown much interest in me, I thought.

I sighed, arose, and returned to Hale Aloha. I was still there when the night came, the moon rose out of the Pacific more majestically than I'd ever dreamed possible, and the plaintive sound of guitars and ukeleles began working their magic on the wind. I'd always heard about the romantic lure of Hawaii's music, but until this moment I hadn't realized how truly beautiful and irresistible it was.

Half berating myself for even thinking of going to the party unescorted, and yet unable to withstand the mystic of the music on the winds, I made my way to the top of the hill overlooking the beach. The singing and stringed instruments blended with the murmur of the surf and the rattling of palm fronds. A full moon cast soft, dark shadows from the trees. Overhead, great white cumulus clouds silently slid across the heavens.

"Meganne?"

Jim Starrett stood a few feet away, peering at me in the moonlight.

"Didn't mean to frighten you," he said. "Going down to join the fun?"

"Well, I . . ."

"Come on!" He reached out and took my hand. I felt a little tingle as he led me to the path along the cliff to the beach below. We joined the crowd, which included K and his date, a pretty Oriental girl who spoke perfect English, Malia and Derek, and about a dozen others whose names I didn't catch. I felt a little miffed that Derek had asked me to attend this event and yet he seemed to be with Malia. But I put it aside and joined in the singing.

After awhile the music faded, the people ate very reddish hot dogs, quite unlike any I'd seen before, fresh pineapple, and roasted marshmallows. The talk turned (as it always did around a campfire when I was a girl) to ghosts and such things.

The voices were loud, especially K's—he was drinking sake, the hot Japanese white wine. "Ho!" he cried, waving the tiny cup of wine, "you Mainland *haoles* want talk da kine ghost story, I tell you some, bruddahs!"

He was off. He spoke of his childhood and Pele, goddess

of the volcanoes. I questioned him about his seriousness and saw he really believed the legends. He also believed in the *menehunes*, the leprechauns of Hawaii. The locals (as everyone called the native islanders) quite obviously took such stories seriously.

I really hadn't intended to get into the discussion, but I asked, "Could these beliefs be cultural? Merely part of the old stories? I mean, I've never heard of Pele and *menehunes* on the Mainland."

K took a quick sip of sake and answered. "Ho! You know people who won't walk under da kine ladders?"

"Yes. But I'm not superstitious."

"Ah!" Derek persisted, rising from where he'd been sitting on a huge coconut that had washed up on the beach, "but millions of people are."

I defended my viewpoint. "But just because some people believe in superstitions doesn't mean they're right."

"Oh?" Derek was rising to the challenge. "Who's to say what's right and what's wrong?"

I thought about that a moment before replying. Then the answer seemed clear. "The established things would be right, proven things like the Bible."

Everyone was watching Derek and me. He leaned across the campfire, Malia's hand resting lightly on his right, bare forearm. "The established things? Astrology has been around thousands of years. Witchcraft was forbidden in the early part of the Old Testament, but it was established. So those things would be proven, by your standards!"

Jim spoke quietly. "I believe Meganne means that the Bible is the established source of faith, and what it teaches is right. If it warns against something, such as witchcraft, that something is wrong." Jim looked straight at Derek, "No one ever wins an argument about such things. Why don't we talk about something else?"

I was pleased that Jim was defending me. Moonlight

augmented the fire in illuminating his face. As he talked, the sullen, withdrawn, and secretive mood so common to him seemed to slip away. For a long moment, his eyes locked with Derek's and there was tension around the circle. K broke it.

"Ho! You ever hear about da kine *kahuna* live near me when I was a keed?"

The conversation turned to the ancient Hawaiian religion, which was still being practiced in the islands. Jim looked at me.

"You want to take a walk?"

I hesitated. I liked the idea, yet I was somehow afraid of being alone with him. "Not right now," I stalled.

Jim nodded curtly and put a couple of marshmallows to roast over the fire on a stick. I turned to the conversation, but just listened. Derek and K were arguing about whether witches and demons were real.

"Both are allegorical," Derek said. "Religious authorities throughout the centuries used such ideas to control the people. Take Joan of Arc. They burned her as a witch and for heresy. Years later, the same church made her a saint. Now which was she? Witch or saint?"

K waved that question aside. "In da kine islands, we don't burn da bruddahs for what they believe!"

"Ah!" Derek pounced on a new thought. "But once these islands were the scene of human sacrifice."

K shook that one off, too. "Long time befoah my ancestors come to da kine islands! But on Mainland, your ancestors had Salem witch trials. No?"

Derek said, "Like you, that was before my ancestors came to America. But the Puritans did hang nineteen men and women, plus 'pressing' one to death, for refusing to enter a plea of guilty or not guilty to witchcraft and sorcery."

Jim said, "Matter of fact, one of those hanged as a sorcerer—not as a witch or being possessed—was the Rev.

George Burroughs. A clergyman."

Derek pursed his lips. "And all because of what people believe and have the power to do."

Jim asked quietly, "But where would we be without our beliefs? It's what we believe that counts. Even love is a form of belief."

"Ho!" K exclaimed, kissing the pretty Oriental girl quickly, "love may be da kine belief, bruddah, but it sure feels good!"

Everyone laughed. The heavy discussion seemed ended. Someone struck a chord on a guitar. The ukulele joined in. Voices were raised in song.

Jim rose abruptly, pulled me to my feet and said, "Let's walk." This time it wasn't a request. Half fearfully, half eagerly, I walked beside him down the beach, just above the surf's ceaseless rolling tongues.

"What do you want on this island, Meganne?"

I hesitated. I was tempted to tell him that right now I wanted to escape with my life, but decided that was a little melodramatic. Instead I said something about getting reacquainted with my aunts.

He stopped beside a small grove of coconut trees, which had grown beside a small inlet. One tree had fallen across a sandy depression in which a fire had been built. Whoever had been there had gone off, leaving the last piece of wood burning weakly above a bed of live coals.

Jim slid over the log, helped me across, and sat down with his back against the tree trunk, his bare feet to the fire. I joined him, not sure what he was thinking or what I should say.

Finally he asked, "What do you want out of life, Meganne?"

I was a little nervous, but I was interested, too. "Oh, the usual things: a home, family, and happiness."

Jim was silent a long time. The only sound was the

crackling of the dying fire, the trade winds in the fronds overhead, and the lap of the sea. It was a strangely beautiful and yet somehow disturbing scene with the shadows of palms and the leaping, living way Jim's and my shadows moved because of the flame in the coals.

Abruptly, Jim shoved himself to his feet and pulled me up. "Let's walk," he said.

But he didn't. He looked at me with dark, brooding eyes and then slowly, tenderly, pulled me to him. He put both hands gently along my cheeks and tilted my head back until the moon shone fully on my face.

"You are beautiful," he said huskily, and kissed me.

I felt my senses reel. I was afraid of this man and yet I was enjoying his kiss. I didn't know much about him, and yet I knew what I needed to know: I was falling in love with him.

Jim released me and dropped his hands. He turned away, walking around the log's end and back onto the open stretch of beach, facing the distant singing.

"Meganne, if you value your life, leave this island!"

I couldn't believe his fiercely whispered words, "What?"

"You heard me! Get away! Quickly!"

I walked toward him but didn't get too close. I was shivering in the warm night. "If you're trying to scare me, Jim, you're doing a good job of it!"

"I'm just trying to save your life, Meganne! I love you, and I want you to be safe! . . . I've been listening and watching enough to know something very strange is going on around here. Somehow, you're involved. Do as I say! Get off this island!"

"Jim!" I cried as he started back toward the others.

He didn't stop. I ran after him and pulled on his arm. He stopped, facing me with the moon full on his dark, brooding features.

"You don't know whether you're fighting flesh and blood

or something other worldly, do you, Meganne? Well, I know! Now, go! While you still can!"

Chapter Thirteen

I didn't sleep much that night. In the morning I awoke again to the sounds made by the little Japanese doves outside my balcony window. I opened my eyes to the grotesque plaster demon grinning evilly at me from the ceiling. Well, I decided, this has gone far enough! I dressed quickly and went down the stairs. I walked to Aunt Marian's room, knocked a couple of times, and when she didn't answer, I opened the door and called softly.

She didn't answer.

I'd never been in her room before. She had pointedly avoided showing it to me when I'd arrived, and I'd never had an occasion to enter since. But now I went in.

"Aunt Marian?" I called again, but when she still didn't answer, I moved inside the doorway and closed it behind me. I wanted a private conversation with her.

Her brass bed was old and ornate. The dark draperies were pulled back to let in the trade winds, but they were not blowing. The oppressive stillness of a *kona* was thick in the old, musty-smelling room. A Bible lay closed on a large, marble-topped stand. A walk-in closet with open doors beckoned. I entered cautiously, calling her name.

Aunt Marian wasn't there, but something else was. There were bookcases with books on witchcraft, satanism, and the occult. I took a quick look at the titles and moved on in disbelief to astrological charts, tarot cards, and a stack of magazines with the signs of the zodiac on the top cover.

There was a small altar with various items, which at first seemed familiar, and then, in a second glance, were strange. There was a round chart with a five pointed star in the middle—a star made with continuous lines as a child learns to draw, but this one had been drawn by an artist. There was a chalice, a white handled dagger or knife, a censor, a wand, some cords, and a container with what appeared to be salt.

I'd never seen the working tools of a witch before, but I had no doubt that's what I was seeing, for propped open against the wall was a witch's handbook.

My heart was doing crazy things, but my body refused to leave the room. I was fascinated at the strange paraphernalia, so out of place in a professing Christian's home.

My eyes moved to the walls of that walk-in closet. There I saw many other drawings, carvings, and insignias. I didn't know what they were called, but I knew they were some sort of hex signs. There were depictions of demons carved in plaster, iron, or wood that grinned fiendishly. The designs were mixed with strange drawings and circles.

I backed out of the room, my heart beating fast. In that instant, I knew that my Aunt Marian was into the occult. I closed the door and hurried out of the room and down the stairs. From some dim part of my memory came the words, "And I beheld Satan fall from heaven as an angel of light."

I was under control when I entered the kitchen. But Aunt Marian wasn't there. I saw her on the screened-in lanai. Her hair was untidy. She still wore her robe.

I walked out to confront her.

"Oh, there you are, Meganne! I thought you'd be down soon," she said. "Here, sit by me. I've poured you a glass of milk."

I wondered how she knew I'd be down soon. Did she sense something in my attitude? Or had she seen me in her room and let me alone, playing some kind of cat-and-mouse game of her own?

I took the glass of milk in my hand, but I didn't feel like drinking it. I held it, looking out across the green expanse of lawn toward the rain forest, which rose out of the black, twisted volcanic rocks that formed the mountains. I could see the black and white cats moving cautiously out of the dense undergrowth. When they were satisfied the way was clear, they moved carefully across the open space toward the house. The black one led the white one.

"Aunt Marian, I need to talk to you."

"I've been expecting you," she replied. She balanced a half papaya in her hand and squeezed lemon juice over it. "Now's as good a time as any to talk, Meganne."

Suddenly, I found myself saying a little prayer for wisdom and guidance. Only a fragment of a verse Tess had quoted flashed into my mind, but I claimed it silently. "If any man lack wisdom, let him ask of God, who gives to all men liberally. . . ."

I said aloud, "Aunt Marian, I've got to say something to you. But let me say it my own way. OK?"

She looked strangely at me and I felt uncomfortable, but I was determined. That was my "cussed streak" coming out, as my father would have said. I continued aloud, "You remember what Reverend Kim said last Sunday about supermarket religion?"

"You mean where someone wanders through life as through a store, taking a little of this and a little of that?"

"Yes. Mixing up things in the shopping cart, Pastor Kim

said, is like trying to choose what we want out of the Bible and leaving what we don't want. Remember?"

Aunt Marian took a bite of papaya and chewed noisily before answering. "I remember all his sermons, Meganne. In this one, he said that you must not compromise with God. Why do you ask?"

"Do you believe that?"

"Of course."

She made it sound as though I was simpleminded for asking. I tried to think how else I could make my point. "Do you believe someone can talk to God who isn't a believer?"

"A believer in what, Meganne? And yes, for Satan himself talked with God as you'll recall from reading Job."

I was stumped again. How could I help her when I knew so little about witchcraft and she knew so much? I was rescued from my dilemma by Ingrid who appeared at the kitchen door. "Your sister isn't feeling well," she announced. "I'd like you to come up to her room, please."

I set down my glass of milk and leaped up, but Aunt Marian stopped me. "I will see how my sister is, Meganne. If we require your services, I'll call you."

The curt dismissal made me angry, but I held my temper and watched them hurry into the gloomy old house. I was frightened, very frightened. My worst fears were coming true. Something had happened to Tess. But how serious was it? And what did that mean to my own life?

The thoughts chased themselves through my mind while the sky outside suddenly grew dark. I glanced out. Immense black clouds were rising over the horizon. An ugly cloud had blocked the sun although the sky was still partially clear.

I couldn't stand the terrible waiting. I moved through the rooms, fighting the feeling of heavy, threatening forces, which seemed somehow alive and more foreboding and evilly-inclined than ever.

I came back to the foot of the stairs, stared up at the closed door, and wondered why Aunt Marian and Ingrid were taking so long. I thought about going up and knocking on Tess's door, but decided not to unnecessarily antagonize Aunt Marian. So I went back into the kitchen to drink my milk.

"You bad cat!" I cried. The white cat had knocked my glass over on the table and was busily lapping up the milk. I didn't even get close before it turned and raced across the open grass to the shelter of the jungle growth. The black cat sat outside on the chaise longue and stared at me with unblinking yellow eyes.

I took some paper towels, went back to the patio, and cleaned up the mess. I rinsed out the glass and thought about pouring myself some more milk when Ingrid reappeared.

"Tess would like to see you, Meganne. Your Aunt Marian said I should ask you to come up."

I turned the empty glass upside down on the counter and followed Ingrid up the stairs to the second floor, wondering and fearing what I'd find in Tess's room.

Chapter Fourteen

Tess was propped up in bed, supported by pillows. She looked very tired. Her hair wasn't combed. She was so fragile looking and old that it scared me. But she smiled and reached out both thin hands to me. I crossed the room quickly and took her hands.

"Are you all right, Aunt Tess?"

Her blue eyes lit up with the lovingness I'd always admired. "Just a little upset stomach, that's all. Now don't you fret."

I was surprised. I'd thought her high blood pressure had been acting up, but as I glanced at Ingrid and she nodded reassuringly, I felt relieved.

Aunt Marian said, "It's nothing serious, I'm sure. However, you'd better not stay long, Meganne."

K called from the foot of the stairs. Aunt Marian told Ingrid to see what he wanted. It was obvious Marian was not going to leave me alone with Tess, and I desperately needed a few words with her. I smiled at Tess and tried to think how I could say all that I'd learned. Without being aware of it, I prayed silently. "Please, Lord! Get her out of here a moment!"

The Lord had answered even before I called, for Ingrid appeared in the doorway. "K says the radio claims this is going to be a bad storm, and he has some questions for you."

Aunt Marian made annoyed sucking sounds through her teeth. "Oh, very well! I'll be right down. Meganne, my sister should rest now."

I got the message, but Tess protested. "Oh, let her stay just a moment longer."

Aunt Marian was reluctant. "Well, just one minute. Ingrid, you stay right here in case my sister needs you."

Ingrid nodded but as soon as Marian's voice was heard at the bottom of the stairs, and then moving toward the kitchen, the nurse looked meaningfully at me. "Excuse me. I have something I must do just now. I'll be back before she is."

The door closed behind the big woman. Tess and I were alone. I turned quickly to that dear old face.

"Aunt Tess, we must get out of here at once! Your life's in great danger!"

"My life is in God's hands. If he wants me now, I am ready. But you, my dear, are too young to die. And you are not ready. Please! Take this and leave Hawaii as quickly as you can!"

She reached inside her nightstand drawer, fumbled with something underneath the marbled top, and pulled out a thick envelope covered with transparent tape. "I've had this there for years, in case of some emergency. There's enough cash to get you to safety."

"But, Aunt Tess, I can't leave you!"

"I am not alone, Meganne, my dear. I have my Lord! Now, take it and leave as soon as you can. Before the storm if possible. If it's a bad one, the bridge will go out again and you'll be trapped here. Now take this and go!"

"I just can't—!"

"You can and you must! Now, put that money out of sight and promise me you'll do as I ask!"

"Aunt Tess, I can't bear to go alone. If I wait a little bit, you may be strong enough to go with me!"

"No, my dear. I won't hear of it."

I tucked the money inside my bra. There was something else I had to know, and quickly. "Aunt Tess, did you get your will changed?"

"Yes, my dear."

"You did?" I was genuinely surprised. "But how?"

She chuckled. "Knowing I couldn't let the lawyer come here, I resorted to a little trickery. You know the day I had Ingrid take me down to the beach in the car?"

It took me a moment to remember. "Yes, but what's that got to do with it?"

The old woman chuckled again. "I'd had Ingrid call ahead to the attorney and ask him to have the papers drawn quietly, then meet me on the beach."

I frowned. "But the only phone around here is in Tutu's house, and that's part of Hale Aloha's party line! She might have been overheard!"

"I doubt it. The fact that the attorney met me and we took care of things shows she wasn't. Someone would have tried to stop us."

"Where's there another phone around here?"

"Why, at our neighbor's, Jim Starrett's."

I groaned. So that's how he knew the urgency of the situation.

Tess interrupted my thoughts. "That also means, Meganne, that if anything happens to me, you and my sister stand to become the surviving heirs. If you outlive her, then in time, you will have everything you should have. In some small way, that will make up for your grandmother's, your mother's, and your years of harassment. But it also means that you must be away from here as quickly as possible. Your life is in danger."

The floorboards squeaked outside. Ingrid was coming back. Quickly I threw my arms around Tess's bony shoulders and hugged her tightly, trying not to cry.

"Good-bye, Meganne, my dear," she whispered. "I love you. Promise me we'll meet in heaven?"

I drew back, the tears no longer under control. "I promise," I whispered. "Oh, Aunt Tess! I love you so much."

"And God and I love you," she said.

Ingrid opened the door slowly. I smiled at her, fought back the tears, and walked blindly down the stairs. By the time I reached the outside of Hale Aloha, I was crying hard.

"Ho!" K's voice brought me up sharply as I neared the property line. "Where do you go so fast, sistah?"

"Oh, K," I managed to say, "My Aunt Tess isn't at all well!"

"She be OK, you bet! You mo' bettah go back inside. *Kona* come. Storm hard this night, you bet!"

That thought forced me to think clearly. "When will the storm break?"

"Radio say 'bout midnight. But who knows for sure? *Kona!*" K looked in the direction of the rising black clouds now mounting above the rain forest. "Soon bridge wash out! Roads go! Cattle drown! Maybe so people, too."

We were interrupted by a scratching sound. We looked at each other and then followed the sounds. Underneath a rusted car hood, resting partly in the oleander hedge between Hale Aloha and Jim Starrett's little house, we saw a pair of white animal feet.

Fascinated but fearful, I bent to look. The skinny white cat was stretched out on its side, having sought shelter under the old metal hood. His forepaws were drawn up tightly under his thin rib cage. His back legs still moved convulsively in a way that showed the cat was in agony. It had scratched a groove in the dirt and weeds.

"Oh, K! That poor little cat! What happened?"

"See the foam around his mouth? Animals froth like that when they've been poisoned. Too bad! We put out rat poison all the time, but this time the poor cat got it!"

I started to reach out in sympathy to the cat, but K stopped me. And in that instant, I remembered the milk Marian had poured for me but I'd found the cat drinking.

I didn't even risk packing all my things. I went to my room, locked the door, and braced it with the chair. Sobbing, brushing tears away, moaning softly to myself, I threw some things into my cosmetic case because it was the smallest thing I had. A few other personal belongings I stuffed into a flight bag. Then I opened the door, peered fearfully down the hallway, and moved quickly through the rapidly falling gloom.

The first drops of rain fell as I eased out the side door and into the yard. I wanted to go see Aunt Tess one more time, but didn't dare. I was scared to death.

I kept to the oleander hedge until I got to the great iron gate. The rain was falling harder now. The sky was the blackest I'd ever seen. Thunder boomed ominously over the ocean, moving closer. Great sheets of lightning brightened the sky with explosive brilliance and then faded into darkness again.

By the lightning flashes, I made my way down the long driveway to the gate. It was locked! Suddenly panicked, I set down my cosmetic case and seized the iron grillwork with both hands. The flight bag slid off my shoulder to my elbow, but the gate didn't even rattle. A key! Maybe there was a key hidden nearby! Desperately I fumbled around likely places in the stone posts supporting the gate, but there was no key.

I don't know what made me turn. Suddenly I whirled around. A lightning flash silhouetted a towering figure in a head covering that resembled pictures I'd seen of a New England fisherman's sou'wester. The face was hidden under the wet brim. The figure raised his arms, and I had the impression of great wings glistening wetly. My common sense told me it was an old military rain poncho, but my emotions swept the logic away.

I tried to step back and came hard up against the unyielding gate. The figure lowered his arms, and I saw that the frightening winged creature was a human being. Then the hands came up again. I caught the glint of something in one hand. I thought it was a knife.

I screamed, let the flight bag slide the rest of the way down my arm, and caught the handle in my palm. I tried to swing the bag at the thing, which moved slowly, silently, toward me. He brushed the bag aside so easily I nearly fell when the handle was jerked from my hand. It fell to the ground.

I screamed, but the thunder drowned the sound so I barely heard it myself. I kicked instinctively at the glistening wet figure's knees, but missed.

Then I turned and ran.

Silently, the figure turned after me, but instantly tripped over the dropped flight bag. I glanced back to see that he had dropped his weapon and was feeling around for it. That gave me a moment's lead. I ran as fast as I could in the warm, hard rain, recalling something Pastor Kim had said in describing the killer in the occult case. I know that's who was chasing me, and I was sure I knew who he was. The terror of that thought spurred me to run faster into the storm.

I don't know how long I slipped, slid, fell, rose, and stumbled on in that blinding rain. I was cut and scratched from things that reached out in the darkness. But still I ran, blindly, aiming only at escaping the man whom I thought was chasing me to kill me.

Finally, my side stitched in pain, my lungs seared with anguished sucking of hot, humid air, and too exhausted to run further, I ran headlong into an old shed. I pushed my way through the tumbled door and collapsed in the driest corner. The roof was a sieve and the single wall construction wasn't much better, but at least the spot where I lay, panting and sobbing, was partly dry.

I tried to listen for my pursuer, but my own loud, half-strangled sobs and the storm drowned out everything else. There was one consolation in that terrible night: it was raining so hard that visibility was cut to zero. The skies seemed to have burst. Never in my life had I seen such vast amounts of rain. The water fell in blinding sheets that seemed almost solid. Even in the lightning flashes the rain washed away the familiar shape of things—trees, fences, hedges, even the great ugly bulk of Hale Aloha. I peered through the cracks of my little shelter for some landmark, but the rain covered everything—almost.

The next lightning flash showed my pursuer. He was standing just yards away, elbows out, hands on hips or perhaps holding his weapon under the shelter of the poncho wings. His sou'wester streamed with the rain. But his face was still invisible in the shadows.

I held my breath, praying for the lightning to come again and fearful it would—and he'd see me. But when it came, he was gone. I sighed and leaned back, then tensed. Where had he gone? Was he approaching my shelter in the blackness?

"Oh, God!" It was a moaning, anguished prayer.

I tried to still my pounding heart, to ease my labored breathing, to think! I sat there against that splintery old building of rusted corrugated iron and wood and thought of nothing except the terrible trouble I was in. There was only one person to help me, the Lord I had ignored the past few years.

"Call upon me in the day of trouble: I will deliver thee, and thou shalt glorify me."

The words leaped into my mind with a clarity that startled me. I could see them on the open pages of my Bible as I'd read them when I first came to Hale Aloha. They were there, silent as the ink in which they'd been printed, and yet somehow they spoke to me in a way I cannot explain.

I stopped sobbing, swallowing hard, thinking. Other words presented themselves mutely: "For we wrestle not against flesh and blood . . . ; wherefore take unto you the whole armor of God."

I began to pray, not in words, but in sounds and the anguish of a soul beyond the ability to form words. But I knew, somewhere, somehow, that Scripture said the Holy Spirit made intercession for us when we didn't know how—in words or anguish. I couldn't remember how it went.

I began to feel a peace in the middle of that storm which was beyond my ability to understand. Yet it came, and the more I poured out my heart in wordless repentance, and sorrow, and genuine contrition, the greater the peace became.

I remembered Tess's words. I confessed my sins, my doubts, my fears, my anger. I asked forgiveness. I accepted that forgiveness. And even deeper peace seeped through me, warming my very being.

I don't know how long it lasted, but when it was past, and I was again aware of the storm and the situation outside the little nook where I was hidden, I had made up my mind.

Slowly, I got to my feet. I'd run off and left the one person in the world who loved me. No matter what happened, I had to go back to her. And somehow, Aunt Tess and I would see it through—with the Lord we both served.

I peered carefully through the diminishing rain. Visibility was nearly normal but great pools of water stood everywhere. The threatening figure in the poncho was gone; at least, I couldn't see him. I took a deep breath, said a quick, silent prayer, and ran through the puddles and across the soggy lawn to the lights of Hale Aloha. I glanced fearfully behind me, but no one was there.

"Oh, Lord! Let Tess be safe! Protect her, please!"

But when I opened the screen door on the back lanai and saw Ingrid's face, I knew something terrible had happened.

She didn't even notice the frightful appearance I made. And I forgot about it instantly as I cried out, "Ingrid! What's happened?"

The big woman's voice was calm. "Where've you been, Meganne? We've been looking for you."

"Why? What happened?"

Ingrid sighed very slowly and quietly. "Your aunt—she's dead."

Chapter Five

"Oh, no!"

"It's true, Meganne, my dear."

Aunt Tess wheeled her chair out from a corner by one of the kitchen windows. Her face was wet with tears.

"Aunt Tess! I thought—" I ran to her and knelt in disbelief beside her, pulling her frail body against my rain-soaked, muddy breast.

After awhile, it hit me. "Aunt Marian?"

"Yes, my dear."

"But you—?"

"Had a slight stomach distress that has passed."

"But—how? What happened to Aunt Marian?"

"Her heart, it seems."

I stood up, my mind bouncing crazily from thought to thought. "But she's never had a heart problem, has she?"

Ingrid looked steadily at me. "She has all the symptoms of a coronary, but there's something wrong."

I felt the touch of fear again. "What do you mean?"

The big woman shrugged. "Come with me."

123

Tess nodded, and I started to follow Ingrid, then stopped. "Aunt Tess, you shouldn't be left alone down here."

"I'll be all right. Go with Ingrid."

I knelt quickly and kissed the old cheek. I whispered, "I couldn't do it, Aunt Tess. I came back to be with you."

She smiled. "That's what I figured when I saw you coming through that door just now."

I started after Ingrid, then turned back to manage a quick smile. "Aunt Tess, you'll be happy to know I've made things right with our Lord."

She smiled and closed her eyes. I knew she was giving a silent prayer of thanks.

As I followed Ingrid up the stairs I asked, "You don't think it was her heart?"

"No, I do not. I think she was murdered."

I stopped dead still. "You what?"

"I can't prove it, not yet. But there's something wrong. I have attended many geriatrics cases. I know a lot about how they die. There is something—I can't put my finger on it—but there is something unusual about your aunt's death that doesn't ring true."

I felt some relief. "Then you don't know that she was murdered?"

"No, I don't, and yet I do. . . . Come, see for yourself."

There was little about Aunt Marian's body to suggest that she wasn't just asleep. I have not often seen death, but Aunt Marian looked much as she always did. Her hair was untidy. Her thin body was covered with a plain white sheet. But her mouth, usually tightly shut in a thin, determined line, was partially open and slightly twisted to one side as though she had died in agony. Death had frozen the contorted movement at the point of highest pain.

I turned away, eyes closed. I was too stunned to cry.

Aunt Marian's open Bible lay on the marble-topped

nightstand. The bathroom door was open and the old-fashioned white enamel tub with clawfeet was visible.

I stepped past Ingrid and opened the door to the walk-in closet. My eyes skimmed everything, but the tarot cards were gone. So were the astrological charts and other items connected to the occult.

"Ingrid?"

"Yes?"

"Did you touch anything?"

"No, not in that closet. Why?"

"You're sure?"

Ingrid's big body tensed with obvious annoyance. I quickly apologized and she relaxed.

"What was Aunt Marian doing this evening before you found her?"

"The usual things. Why?"

"Nothing unusual?"

The crispness in her voice showed she resented my direct questions. "No, Meganne! Nothing unusual!"

I tried to soften my voice. Patting the big woman's solid arms, I said, "Ingrid, I'm still in shock, I guess. Forgive me for being tactless."

I led the way out the door, glancing again at the walk-in closet. Then, remembering something, I quickly returned and peered inside at the ceiling's strange mixture of drawings, carvings, and insignias. There had been an obvious attempt to break, deface, or remove the signs.

I walked out of the closet and back to the dark door where Ingrid was waiting for me.

When we reached the bottom of the stairs, Tess was sitting there in her wheelchair. I threw my arms around her.

"I can't tell you how sorry I am," I said.

She shook my sympathies off with determination. "Did you find any evidence she was murdered?"

I glanced at Ingrid, who shrugged. "No," I said. "But we didn't examine—the body."

"You must!" Tess's firmness surprised me. It was as though she'd had a strong determination under her quiet, subservient manner, and now that her dominant sister was dead, Tess's strength was beginning to come out.

I knelt by her and took her blue-veined, thin hands in mine. "Tess, why are you so determined to have us do something we know nothing about?"

Tess's blue eyes were firm and met mine steadily. "Because neither the doctor nor the mortician can get in here for a while. The radio said everything was washed out or closed by landslides and debris, so it'll be at least sometime tomorrow."

Her voice was rising slightly with her intensity. She took a deep breath and continued. "Ingrid has said a very serious thing; I hardly believe that my sister was murdered, but so many strange things have happened recently that we must do what we can to find out. Oh, Meganne, don't you see that?"

I squeezed her hand. "Yes, Tess. I see that." I stood up and faced Ingrid. "Do you have something specific to go on, or are you guessing?"

Ingrid took a slow breath. "I have seen people die before. I've spent my life working with old people. I believe your aunt was murdered." Ingrid reached into her pocket and brought out something in a closed fist. She extended her hand, palm up.

I reached for the little clear glass vial. "That's the high blood pressure medication the doctor prescribed for Tess. I'm not sure what you're trying to tell us."

Ingrid reached into her pocket with the other hand and brought out a small plastic hypodermic syringe. "Do you understand now?" she asked.

Tess and I glanced at each other and shook our heads.

"I found this empty vial outside Marian's door when I went to check on her about an hour ago. I picked it up, thinking it had been accidentally dropped from the medicine tray."

Ingrid paused as though we should understand, but again Tess and I shook our heads. "When she didn't answer my knock, I opened the door and peeked in. This syringe was just inside, on the floor."

Somewhere in the back of my mind a glow of light began. "And then?" I asked with rising excitement.

"I picked up the syringe, turned on the light, and saw she was very still. I checked her pulse and knew she was dead."

Tess protested, "I don't see what that has to do with those things," she indicated the vial and syringe.

"I think I'm beginning to see it," I said slowly, feeling the fear rise in my throat. "Aunt Marian wasn't on that medication. It's yours, Tess. Someone went into Aunt Marian's room and used that medication to kill her—with the syringe—since you take that orally and not with injection."

"Exactly!" Ingrid cried. "If this oral medication is injected, it produces cardiac arrest symptoms. In fact, it simulates them so perfectly that the truth isn't usually suspected, and no autopsy is performed."

"If someone wanted to kill Aunt Marian that way, why leave evidence to indicate it might be murder? The killer wouldn't be so careless as to leave two clues—one, maybe—but not two! No, Ingrid! It doesn't make sense!"

"Unless," Tess said very slowly, her left hand going up to touch her chin in thought, "the murderer wanted to make it look as though someone else had done it."

"Red herrings!" I cried, remembering the term my father had used. Then I remembered something else and turned to Ingrid. "But if there was an injection, wouldn't there be evidence of that?"

"I looked," Ingrid admitted. "But I couldn't find any

signs of a hypodermic injection. . . . There's one place I forget to check, though." She turned with surprising agility and hurried up the stairs.

"Tess," I said softly, again kneeling by the old woman, "I'm sorry about all this. It's bad enough to lose your sister, but to suspect she was murdered—that's terrible!"

The old woman's blue eyes clouded with pain. "I can live with such things, Meganne. What I cannot bear is to know that she might not have had time to make her peace with God."

I looked thoughtfully at Tess. I knew without asking that she had known about her sister's involvement in the occult as well as her terrible years of hatred.

"Maybe she did," I said hopefully.

Tess began to cry. "To go into the presence of God without being right in this life is the worst thing that could happen. You know that, Meganne."

"Tess, what did Aunt Marian do this evening? Think carefully!"

"What on earth for, Meganne? She's dead!"

"Please, Tess!"

The old woman frowned and began to think. She told of Aunt Marian's last hours in bits and pieces, injecting new facts as she remembered them. I waited anxiously, not wanting to put false hopes into Tess's heart until I had something tangible to go on, not just a wild hope.

When she had finished, I reviewed things. "When Aunt Marian knew the storm was coming, she sent everyone home so they'd not be caught in the rain. But first she had K bring her a hammer and she went upstairs for a while after everyone was gone. Then you heard muffled pounding?"

"Yes," Tess said, frowning up at me as my excitement arose.

"Later, Aunt Marian came downstairs while the storm

was at its highest and burned something over there in the fireplace?" I walked over to the huge opening and knelt. There were only charred bits of paper; nothing I could see that showed what those items had been.

"Yes," Tess said, wheeling her chair closer to me and the fireplace. "But I don't know what you're thinking, Meganne."

"Why should she burn anything on a hot, humid night when the *konas* are blowing and a storm is keeping everyone away from this house?" I demanded.

"I asked her," Tess said, "and she naturally told me it didn't concern me."

"Think back!" I urged, running my forefinger through the charred papers, which floated in tiny flakes up the chimney. "Think back! Did she say or do anything unusual before that?"

Tess frowned deeply. "Well, now that you mention it, she did do something she hasn't done in so many years I can't remember."

"What was that?"

"She kissed me."

"Aunt Marian kissed you, Tess?"

"Yes. She had been reading her Bible, and then she seemed to be praying for quite a while. But she doesn't like to be disturbed, you know, so I didn't think anything of it. She's the only person I ever knew who could hate and read and pray, maybe all at once. But she did surprise me when she walked by, patted me on the arm, and kissed me on the cheek. Right here."

I looked at the right cheek where Tess's thin finger was resting. "You know what?" I asked, and then didn't wait for an answer, "I think Aunt Marian was touched by God's Holy Spirit, and she went upstairs, tried to destroy all those—"

I stopped, unsure if Tess really knew, but she nodded and

said, "You mean those pagan symbols and pictures she had in her closet?"

"Yes," I said. "I just saw where all her occult charts, symbols, and tarot cards were gone!"

"You mean," Tess said slowly, reaching out to me, "you think maybe she burned them?"

"What else could it be?"

"But why, Meganne?"

"I can only think of one reason. God really touched her life, and she was beginning to clean up her misbeliefs by destroying the obvious signs."

"Oh, Meganne! Don't fool an old woman like me with false hopes!"

"I'm not fooling you, Tess! I can't think of any other reason for Aunt Marian to have acted the way she did. Can you?"

Tess was thoughtful for a moment. Then her old wrinkled face began to break into a smile. "She did change, didn't she, Meganne?"

Ingrid came back down the stairs.

She called, "I found it!"

"Found what?" I asked.

"The puncture wound. Inside the roof of her mouth. I'm sure an autopsy will confirm she was murdered!"

Tess and I glanced at each other with sudden understanding.

"Then that means," I said fearfully, "somebody killed Aunt Marian and—" I left the words unsaid, but I could see Tess understood.

"And the murderer may still be in this house," Tess said softly.

Chapter Sixteen

Even though Tess had said it quietly, the impact was tremendous. I glanced at Ingrid. Big and strong as she was, she showed very human signs of fear. She licked her lips and I heard her tongue click in her mouth because it had suddenly gone dry. As for myself, I felt something invisible, but strong, gripping my throat from the inside so that I was having trouble breathing. Only Tess seemed relatively at ease.

She was the first to speak again. "But on second thought, that's highly unlikely. The first logical thing a murderer would do is get away."

My heart had jumped with relief at first, but her last words punctured my hope and fear surged in to replace it. "Up until you said, 'logical,' Tess, I thought you were right. But there's a lot around this place that isn't logical."

Tess looked at me with surprise. "Are you talking about demons and such things, Meganne?"

"No," I said honestly, "but if Ingrid's right and Aunt Marian was murdered, why would the killer leave evidence around to show it hadn't been a heart attack?"

Tess said eventually, "That's easy. The medication is mine. I sometimes have injections. . . . Perhaps someone is trying to make it look as though I'm responsible for my sister's death."

"That's crazy!" I cried. "Anyone knows you're the sweetest person in the world!"

"I'm just saying," Tess mused, "that someone might have thought to place the blame on me. If he's that clever, more evidence might have been planted to implicate me."

"Or she," Ingrid said.

I had been going to jump on Tess's remark and rebuke her, but Ingrid's quick, short reply made me stop and blink. "What did you say?"

The big woman cocked her head. "No offense, Meganne, but it could have been a woman and not a man who murdered your aunt."

I was hurt and angry, so I lashed out without thinking. "You think maybe I wasn't caught out there in that storm?"

"I don't think anything," Ingrid said a little stiffly. "I'm just saying that either a man or a woman could have killed your aunt."

I had to stop myself from saying more, because Ingrid was right. But the thought crossed my mind that *she* could have been the one to inject the medication. After all, how did I know she'd found the vial and syringe as she claimed? It gave me a funny feeling.

Tess came to my rescue. "We're all so jumpy we're saying and doing the wrong things! Ingrid, we have only your opinion that my sister was the victim of foul play. No, wait! Don't interrupt! I will not argue with your conclusion at this point. If you're right, we're all in danger. If you're wrong, no harm will have been done by protecting ourselves. Now, let's consider what we should do, after we pray."

She bowed her head and said a short, earnest prayer. I bowed mine slightly, as did Ingrid, but I kept my eyes open and noticed Ingrid had done the same. After Tess said, "Amen," she looked up from her wheelchair and smiled.

"I have asked for God's wisdom," she said. "Now, assuming that Ingrid is right, what must we know to protect ourselves?"

I remembered the stories my father had written in his newspaper days. "Motive," I said, "and opportunity."

Ingrid frowned, not following me, but Tess's blue eyes lit up. "I wouldn't have used those exact terms, my dear, but they make sense. Now, while we're together, let's consider possible motives, and think who could have been in this house tonight."

Immediately Tess and I knew the obvious.

"Someone must know you changed your will!" I said softly.

Ingrid interrupted before Tess could answer. "What difference would that make?"

"Plenty," I said. "Aunt Tess, who besides your attorney knew your will was changed?"

The old woman frowned. "Why do you ask that?"

"Because," I said, keeping my voice low in case someone was in the house that we didn't know about, "when you changed your will, and Aunt Marian died, you became the sole recipient of the entire estate. Right?"

"Under the original terms the surviving sister inherited everything, yes. But I don't see . . ."

I interrupted. "And under the terms of your revised will, it anything happens to you, the entire estate would not go to Malia, as before, but to me. Right?"

"Yes." She said it in such a way that I knew she hadn't understood. But Ingrid did.

"Meganne means that not only is your life in danger, Tess, but so is hers, because if both of you were dead, the terms of the original will would prevail!"

Aunt Tess's frown deepened. "Well, I don't know, but I suppose so. But surely you're not suggesting that Malia would be involved in such a terrible thing?"

"We're not saying she is," I explained. "It could be somebody else who stands to benefit through Malia. We simply don't know, but we can't take a chance."

"I've known Malia for years," Tess mused. "She wouldn't do such a thing. Although . . ." she hesitated, looking at me, "she is involved in witchcraft."

Tess paused, then said, "Obviously someone who is into witchcraft is separated from God, for his Word clearly shows that he forbids its practice. The logical question, of course, is: would such a person be capable of murder?"

I didn't know what to think. But I remembered an old saying or something about 'poison is a woman's weapon.' Aloud, I said, "No matter what the circumstances, Aunt Tess, it's common sense for you and I to consider ourselves possible targets. Because Ingrid here is positive . . ." A thought hit me, and my voice trailed off.

But Ingrid understood. She stiffened momentarily, and then controlled her emotions. "Ah, *liebchen!* You're thinking suspiciously, I see! Your thoughts are in your face. Even if Malia was guilty, she might not have acted alone against your dead aunt; so? You think, 'how does Ingrid know this particular medication is deadly only by injection, and who would know to make such an injection in the roof of the mouth? Who, indeed!"

"Ingrid, I didn't mean . . ."

The big woman stopped me with an impatient wave. "It is nothing! I understand your reasoning. Well, let me tell you something. I have worked around doctors all my life. When they're not around patients, they talk about all sorts of things, especially at lunch or on a coffee break. One time, I heard a doctor tell how he had a case such as this. I thought of that, and checked your aunt, and it is the same. But let me tell you one more thing, *liebchen!* If I were the one who had killed your Aunt Marian that way, would I be so stupid as to reveal my method?"

I took a quick step and laid my hand on Ingrid's large forearm, which she had folded defiantly across her substantial bosom. "Ingrid, what can I say? I'm so sorry!"

There was understanding in Ingrid's eyes. "It is nothing! Forget it! Now, let's think about our safety. Yes," she repeated, seeing me glance sharply at her, "our safety! For if it is important to whoever murdered your Aunt Marian to remove you too, perhaps I will also be a target."

"Not that I believe anyone is actually going to do such a thing," Aunt Tess said, "But we must all stay together. Sooner or later, the men will come—K, especially—and we'll be safe once the phones are restored to service."

I glanced around the room. Whoever had chased me from the gate in the rain was probably still out there, perhaps watching. But even if I closed all the windows and bolted every door, he might have already entered the house and be hiding. I felt my skin prickle with the thought.

Suddenly, I saw Ingrid stiffen with alarm.

"What is it, Ingrid?" I asked tensely.

The big woman sniffed the air. "Smoke! I smell smoke!"

I glanced at the fireplace. There was no hint of smoke there, but now I smelled it, too.

"Upstairs," Ingrid said, starting for the stairs. "I think it's coming from there!"

My eyes caught a flash of flame from the kitchen. The yellow orange flicker reflected from the walls. "No!" I cried, pointing, "there!"

Instantly, Ingrid turned from the stairs and ran for the kitchen. I started after her, but she called, "No, I can handle it! You stay with Tess." Ingrid was already through the room and into the kitchen.

"Meganne! Look! Where is that smoke coming from?"

I looked where Tess's finger was pointing. Smoke was clearly drifting down the stairs.

"Oh, no!" I cried, and raced up the stairs, my heart pounding. I reached the top of the stairs to see smoke hanging in the still air of the long hallway, shifting ever so slightly as though it were alive.

My eyes followed it up. The smoke was coming from the attic. I scurried fearfully toward the open door to my room.

In a moment, I stood panting, one hand clutching the doorframe. There I saw a tongue of flame reflected outside the door to the balcony. I rushed toward the screen, slid it open without thinking, and saw the flames. Lightning had struck the balcony, I thought.

Two things happened at once. I realized that the flames were from a bucket sitting in the middle of the balcony, and I heard the door slam behind me and the lock turn.

Chapter Seventeen

I tugged frantically at the wooden door that led back into the house, but it was locked.

I was trapped!

In that instant, my frenzied mind grasped the horrible significance of what had happened. Tess was alone in her wheelchair. Ingrid was behind a closed door in the kitchen. Maybe she, too, had found a bucket of smoking, burning rags.

It was so deliberate a trap that I kicked myself mentally for having fallen into it. But there was no time for berating myself. I jerked and tugged and shoved on that heavy door, but it only rattled at my frantic efforts. I skirted the fire in the bucket and leaned over the railing.

It was at least a thirty-foot drop to the ground, and that was within a few feet of the edge of the cliff. Even if I could jump and not hurt myself, I'd probably lose my balance and hit the wooden guardrail. If I broke through that, it was a drop of several hundred feet to the beach below. That was sure death!

Desperately I leaned forward to see if there was some foothold below the balcony where I could work my way down through the darkness. I couldn't see a thing, although I could hear the distant booming of the surf.

Sobbing at my desperate situation and fearing for Tess's life, I scurried along the metal balcony railing, leaning far over to peer frantically into the night, hoping for some way to escape. The light inside my room snapped off and total blackness engulfed me.

I heard a sound behind me and started to turn, but someone grabbed me. Before I could scream, I was lifted bodily from the wooden floor of the balcony and shoved violently over the railing into the darkness below.

I grabbed for the railing, partially caught it with my right hand, but was not able to save myself. I felt my fingernails breaking off and searing pain ripped the flesh along my arms. In that terrible moment I tried to grip something with my left hand, but touched only the empty night air beneath the balcony. I screamed as splinters tore through my hand, and then I fell through the night, kicking and clutching.

I hit something hard. A shock of pain punctured my body, but I grabbed out blindly and held on as I collapsed onto something solid, stunned and semiconscious.

I felt gingerly around in the darkness and realized I'd fallen onto the edge of one of the many-angled roofs of the Victorian mansion. I hurt all over, but my fright was greater than my pain. I reached out until I found the edge of the roof.

Instinctively, I leaned toward the main bulk of the house, trying to clear my brain. I moved my right leg. It didn't seem broken. I could feel warm stickiness on my hands and knew I was bleeding. But I was alive! I muttered, "Thank you, Father!" and then began to pray in earnest.

My eyes had become accustomed to the night so I could see vague shadows and forms. I was on a tiny piece of the second-story roof, which jutted out at an angle to join the main roof.

No one was likely to come looking for me. All that mattered now was to stay alive, so that I could get back downstairs to save Aunt Tess. If I was supposedly dead, killed falling off the balcony from my room, then Tess was next. And she was alone and terribly vulnerable!

"Please, Lord! I didn't come this far to fail now!"

I worked my way down from the second story roof. If I lowered myself full-length by the rainspout—and it didn't pull loose—I'd only be ten or fifteen feet from the ground. It was soft from the storm, which had almost past.

With another quick prayer, I lowered myself, fighting with all my strength to hold on until I was dangling my feet in nothingness and my arms were about to be pulled from their sockets as I clung desperately to the spout overhead.

I looked once more to see my landing spot in the darkness. From a slice of yellow light reflecting out the window below, I could see a clump of ti leaves. They wouldn't be hard to land on. In fact, they'd help.

Then I saw something else. The black cat's eyes reflected the house light. He was watching me, but the rest of his body was lost in the night. Instinctively, I started trying to pull myself up. To my frantic mind, that black cat represented evil triumphant.

Stop it, Meganne! You're being melodramatic again! Now, let go and that cat will run from you. 'Face the devil and he will flee from you!'

I let go with my fingers. I landed in a tangle of wet ti leaves. But no pain shot through my body; I hadn't broken or twisted anything. And I was already so scratched and cut and wet that a little more didn't bother me.

I stood up, brushing myself off. The black cat had moved a few feet away, but he was still glaring balefully at me with eyes that seemed to fill the night.

"Shoo!" I waved my wet, bleeding hands at him. He turned away. The eyes vanished, but now I could see the cat's black body. He scampered through a be-still tree's lower branches where they trailed the ground. Then he let out a little squeal, bounded sideways into the window's light, and stood there, shaking his forepaw.

Whatever had touched him seemed to glint like wire. But it wasn't wire; it was much too thin. The cat shook his paw again. Instantly, something crashed inside the house. The cat sprang away in fright and vanished into a hole under the mansion.

I was desperate to reach Tess, but I stopped to pick up the glistening thread, which had snagged the cat's forepaw. I held the object up to the light—and almost cried out with relief!

Then horrible realization hit me. That was Derek's nearly invisible fishing line! That was how the radio seemed to jump off the shelf, and my perfume bottle, and whatever had crashed inside the house just now.

It was Derek, not Jim! Derek was the enemy.

But how could I deal with him?

I didn't know; all I knew was that if I could get to Tess in time, I might save her life.

I ran, sobbing with fear, around the side of Hale Aloha and into the screened-in back lanai. Quickly and quietly, I slipped into the house and ran across to the kitchen.

The bucket was in the sink. Steam still rose from it although Ingrid had doused the fire. She had been tricked as I had. But did that mean she had also been attacked?

Still without a plan, but anxious to save Tess by my presence if nothing else, I gently opened the door where I'd last seen her.

Tess was slumped sideways in her wheelchair, her right arm dangling over the spokes. And towering above her, a heavy fireplace poker in her right hand, was—Ingrid!

Chapter Eighteen

Without thinking, I shoved the door wide and stepped through. "Ingrid! You've killed her!"

The nurse turned slowly toward me. She moved the poker in her hand. Her eyes stared at me strangely. I knew I must look a fright—with bleeding hands and torn clothes, plus the mud I'd picked up—but that wasn't what she was seeing.

I advanced toward her, angry and filled with strength and determination I didn't know was in me. "Get back! Let me see her!"

Slowly, Ingrid obeyed. She took a half-step backward, the poker still gripped in her strong right hand. I kept a wary eye on that while moving quickly but carefully to Tess's side. I dropped to my muddy knees beside that dear, gray head and touched the dangling arm, which had fallen over the wheelchair's side.

The gray hair had fallen across her wrinkled face, but as I bent close I thought for one wild, joyful moment I'd seen a bright blue eye behind the hair. Then I saw the blood.

She'd been hit across the right side of her head and had fallen to the right, hiding the wound until I was close to her.

"Oh, Tess!" I moaned. I wanted to take that precious old head in my arms, but common sense and logic stopped me. I stood up quickly and stood facing Ingrid.

"Give me the poker, Ingrid."

To my surprise, she obeyed my quiet, determined voice. She held the terrible instrument out so the bloody end nearly touched me. I drew back instinctively and then stepped warily forward so I could grip the poker about halfway up. I jerked it from her lax fingers and stepped back, moving my own hand up to the handle where I now had a weapon between us.

"Why, Ingrid?" I cried. "Why?"

She stared at me. "Why, what?"

"You know what!" I yelled, brandishing the poker as menacingly as I could. "Why did you kill my Aunt Tess?"

Ingrid blinked and stepped back as though I'd hit her with the poker. "Wha-a-at?" she stammered. "I didn't kill her!" Then realization came flooding back into her eyes, and she turned her face away from me so I could see the back of her head. It was bloody.

"It wasn't really a fire, Meganne," Ingrid explained. "It was only a bucket of old rags smoking. I put it in the kitchen sink. While I was doing that, someone hit me—here." She gingerly touched her head.

"I didn't see or hear anything. I was out cold on the kitchen floor when I came to, all bloody. I just now came into this room and saw your aunt like this. I—I didn't think, but just reached down and picked up the poker."

For a moment, I didn't know what to do. I looked hard at her. She could be lying. She could have followed me upstairs. She was certainly strong enough to have thrown me off the balcony.

I shook my head, trying to clear the swirling fog of thoughts. "Ingrid, I don't know whether to believe you or not."

Her eyes widened and she sucked her breath in sharply. It was an old trick. I'd seen enough movies and television to know I was supposed to whirl around to see what she pretended to see, and then she'd grab the poker. I started to tell her that, but a voice behind me said quietly, "Believe her, Meganne."

I turned. "Derek! So it was you!"

Derek Norton leaned against the inside of the open door, which separated the big dining room from the kitchen. He was completely calm. I remembered what my father had said during his newspaper days on a police beat. "Cops think they have a sixth sense, but it's really more a great skill to read body language and little, subtle signs. A normal, scared person gets a dry mouth, talks and acts nervous; a person who doesn't exhibit those actions and attitudes, who's too cool, too calm, is the one to watch out for."

Derek held no weapon, but he obviously felt he controlled Ingrid and me with something I couldn't see.

He was still frowning. "What do you mean, 'So it was you!'?"

My own mouth was full of invisible sand. "I found your fishing line; rather, the black cat did."

"What?"

"I saw how you've been making radios fall off shelves to electrocute people."

Derek chuckled. "Oh, that! Do I make a pretty good poltergeist, Meganne?"

"Good enough," I admitted.

A wave of sickness swept through me as I thought of something else. "It was you out there in the storm, wasn't it? In the sou'wester and the poncho?"

"You were luckier than the others, San Francisco!"

I started to ask, "Which others?" but didn't. I remembered the pastor's sermon and his remarks about the winged devil some witnesses had seen at the scene of at least one occult murder. I shuddered hard. "You were very clever, Derek. The arrow—you shot it to scare me, and then pulled the arrow out with your fishline attached to the shaft. Right?"

"Give the little lady a cigar!"

"And the tarot card of death, you stuck that on my door. You did it all, didn't you?"

"Right again, San Francisco! All of it. At the same time I tried to blame it on Starrett."

Derek laughed. "Yes, I do make a pretty good poltergeist; don't I? Just slip into the room when nobody's around, attach the line, and feed it out carefully—well hidden—and then pull at the right time. Presto! Alakazam! The object leaps, my line is retrieved—unseen by human eye because the eye is looking at the fallen object—and nobody suspects a thing! You'd never have caught on if that stupid cat hadn't got tangled up in one of my lines! Pretty clever, huh, San Francisco? Like stepping close to the wall in those old hallways—the floors won't squeak. Fooled everyone, didn't I?"

My mind was spurting off in all directions, a trapped creature desperately seeking escape. I had nothing to hope for, but as long as I was alive, there was a chance.

"You sure had me fooled," I admitted.

Derek grinned happily. "I fool them all. It's easy because nobody ever suspects me of anything." His face clouded. "I . . . hey! What's she doing?"

My eyes followed his to Ingrid. She looked very pale. Gingerly, she started to reach for her wounded head, but she didn't make it. Slowly, she began easing toward the floor.

"Ingrid!" I said, but she went on down, her knees slowly

buckling and her big body melting into the floor.

I turned on Derek with anger. "You've killed her, too!"

"I tried," he admitted, looking at the poker in my hands. "The old lady was easy. But that big gal has a harder head than I thought."

"But why?" I pleaded. "What possible reason?"

He shrugged and gingerly touched his sunburned nose. "Who needs a reason?" He seemed to think about that and pursed his lips.

I stared at him and my entire body turned to goose-bumps. "What're you saying?"

"Why does there always have to be a motive? Your logical mind says I was after marrying Malia so I could inherit this ugly old place through her, along with the pineapple and sugarcane plantations their conglomerate owns. That's what you would think, isn't it?"

I nodded. "Yes. That's logical."

Derek smiled. "Why do something logical? Why not do something just because I wanted to?"

"Like scaring two old ladies to death?"

Again, the shrug. "It started out that way. Then it wasn't much fun, because the oldest one wouldn't admit to anyone that things were happening to her, and that one," he indicated Tess's still form, "went on calmly, talking about being ready to meet her Maker and even about how happy she would be to get to heaven. So I just helped them along, that's all."

I couldn't believe my senses. Here was a man calmly leaning against a door and discussing violence without motives, terror without reason, and enjoying it. He's crazy! I told myself. Stark, raving mad! And I'm the only one he's attacked who's still alive. He can't allow that to happen. He couldn't let me live. I knew that, but instead of being full of goosebumps again, I was reasonably calm. I still had the poker in my hand, and if I could strike—

Derek read my mind. "Drop the poker, Meganne!"

I began to back up, slowly, moving the poker back out of Derek's reach.

He lost his cool. Anger flashed across his face. He shoved himself away from the wall and moved toward me, deliberately, calmly.

I backed up until my legs touched Ingrid's form. I turned sideways, watching Derek, holding onto the poker, and backed toward the wheelchair, hoping I would reach the hall door. Maybe if I could get through it, and slam it . . .

"I'm tired of waiting, Meganne. Now, you hand me that poker, or drop it on the floor right now. Then I'm going to be on my way."

Derek came toward me. "You would have been better off dying when you went over the railing. The bottom of the cliff would have saved you all this." He kept coming, slowly. His eyes went to the doorway behind me. He knew what I planned.

That's when I knew I had to try something unexpected. Derek's purpose was more menacing now.

Suddenly, surprising even myself, I raised the poker and jumped at him. He instinctively backed up, tripped over Ingrid's big form, and fell hard. I screeched and leaped toward him before he could scramble to his feet, but I didn't have to use the poker.

K and Jim dashed through the kitchen door and leaped upon Derek while he was still on his hands and knees. There was a brief, violent scuffle, and I stepped back, suddenly weak in the knees. The poker fell from my hands. I collapsed beside the wheelchair and took that dear old saint's thin, blue-veined hand in mine. I held it to my cheek and cried.

"Meganne?"

I started. Tess's gray head moved. She raised up slowly in the wheelchair. "I didn't know what else to do," she said weakly, "so I just pretended. . . ."

I threw myself, muddy clothes and all, upon the sweet old woman and crushed her to myself. I held her tight until Jim and K finished tying Derek with a piece of his own shirt. Then they checked Aunt Tess and Ingrid and determined they weren't seriously injured. At last the tension eased and K turned to grin at me.

"Ho!" he exclaimed, wiping his brow. "Good thing Jim and I see each other and talk about you *pupule* Mainland *wahine*, you bet!" K shook his head and glanced at the sullen, silent figure bound on the floor. "That, he pupule, foh sure! But that Jim—ho!—he very akamai!"

Jim explained quietly, a hint of a smile at the end of his mouth. "K says you're a 'crazy woman' from the Mainland, and I'm smart, but I think you're the smart one, Meganne."

K cried, "Good thing we smell dat smoke, sistah, and come look-see! We get here just in time, you bet! *Pupule wahine!*"

Jim said soberly to K, "You can't talk about the *he wahine u 'i* that way, K!"

"Ho! You call her a beautiful woman! I call her *pupule!*"

"You're not crazy, are you Meganne?" Jim asked, coming close.

I lowered my eyes. "Jim, I can't tell you how sorry I am about misjudging you!"

"It's OK, darling," Jim said huskily, and pulled me to him.

I protested, "I'm a mess!"

K laughed. "Ho! You a live mess, sistah! That's da nicest *kine!*"

Jim encircled me with his arms. It was the best feeling in the world. But I still couldn't understand something that was bothering me very much. I asked, "How could anyone do such a terrible thing for no reason, Jim?"

He didn't let go, but looked at Derek. "You missed something about Derek. He talked a big game, but he really had plenty of reason to strike down your aunts and you. If you think he was—well, possessed—forget it!"

I looked up at Jim. His craggy features softened, and he barely said the words aloud, but I heard them clearly.

"Derek stood to inherit Hale Aloha if he married Malia, and she was sole heir to this place. But you complicated it when your Aunt Tess wanted to name you as the legal heir."

"So," I said slowly, "it was greed, after all?"

"Mostly, yes; but from what K has told me, Malia was losing her power over your Aunt Marian. In her old age, your aunt was having second thoughts about witchcraft. She'd used contacts in the coven to have Mainland covens spread the rumors that harmed your mother's life and yours. But when Malia told Derek that your Aunt Marian was thinking of getting out—"

I glanced at Aunt Tess. There were tears in her eyes. I knew what she was thinking. Aunt Marian had made her peace with God and destroyed her symbols of evil shortly before Derek had killed her.

"Ho!" K cried, "Malia got planty scared, you bet! She tell me Derek threaten her! Maybe she so scared she give up her *pupule* ideas; maybeso marry good local *kane*; have planty keeds! Now, Jim, you going to *honi* dat Mainland *wahine*, or do I got do it for you, bruddah?"

"*Mahalo nui loa*, K," Jim said with a grin, "thank you very much, but I can do my own kissing."

And he did.

That was a long time ago. Aunt Tess and Ingrid recovered from their injuries. Both women saw Jim and me married. Both fussed over our first child. Tess is gone now; she's with her Lord. But she lived long enough to see her prayers answered, and I'm grateful for that.

We had Hale Aloha painted a cheerful white with green trim. K still manages the place and Ingrid is the housekeeper. Tutu and her husband rest in a little covered cemetery near the Koolau rain forests. Malia married and moved to one of the neighboring islands and I lost track of her. But not before one final, tragic event.

Derek escaped from the mental institution where he had been confined. He quarreled with Malia on the spot where Tess's nurse had fallen to her death. Derek tripped over the black cat, which tried to run between Malia and Derek as they struggled. He lost his balance and died as Alema had.

Jim and I are active in our church here in California's Mother Lode country. Jim's books are selling reasonably well, and he's a wonderful husband and father.

Sometimes we return to Hale Aloha, for it is now truly a house of love. But then so is our little mountain home in California, far away from Hawaii, but very close to God.